BANSHEES OF
ST BRIGID'S

BANSHEES OF
ST BRIGID'S

GERI VALENTINE

POOLBEG

Published 1996 by
Poolbeg Press Ltd,
123 Baldoyle Industrial Estate,
Dublin 13, Ireland

© Geri Valentine 1996

The moral right of the author has been asserted.

A catalogue record for this book is available from the British Library.

ISBN 1 85371 637 5

Cover illustration by Marie Louise Fitzpatrick
Cover design by Poolbeg Group Services Ltd
Set by Poolbeg Group Services Ltd in Stone 9.5/14
Printed and bound in Great Britain by
Cox & Wyman Ltd, Reading, Berks.

About the Author

Geri Valentine was born in Dublin and now lives near Dundalk, Co Louth. *Banshees of St Brigid's* is her fifth book in the hugely successful St Brigid series.

Also by Geri Valentine

Bad Habits at St Brigid's

New Broom at St Brigid's

St Brigid's Bounces Back

Buon Giorno St Brigid's

Published by Poolbeg

To Iseult, Alter Ipse Amicus

Contents

1

Once Upon a Time

One calm night in the Autumn of 1896, as the harvest moon rode high in the heavens illuminating the castle of St Brigid's, slumbering peacefully by the dark waters of the river Boyne, six masked figures, slipping along like shadows, went swiftly up the narrow stone stairs of the east tower.

On reaching the door at the top of the staircase, their leader paused before pushing it slowly open. Holding her candle high in front of her, she peered cautiously into the pitch dark room before entering it.

"Come on," she whispered softly back to her friends. "Everything is just the same as we left it."

They scurried in behind her, quickly seating themselves on upturned boxes which formed a circle in the middle of the room. Their leader carefully placed her candle, in its white candlestick, on the floor between them where it cast a small pool of light, making the surrounding darkness appear even denser.

"What a horrid clanging noise that school clock makes," grumbled one of the group. "It nearly deafened me, banging away all over the place."

"Oh Jane, you know that's only because we are so near to it up here," explained her neighbour, a girl called Anne.

Jane ignored her and said fretfully "Are you sure, Lizzie, that it's safe tonight? I had a terrible feeling that something was following us."

"Probably Clement," retorted Lizzie laughing "You know he wanders all over the place at night."

The rest of the group groaned at this. Clement, an enormous bad tempered tom-cat with mean green eyes, a special favourite of Sr Bernard the headmistress, was extremely unpopular with the girls.

"How could you, Lizzie, you know how I abominate that cat," protested Rosa, a diminutive girl who sat very straight and upright on her box. "I'm convinced he spies on us and reports everything back to Sr Bernard."

A ripple of laughter greeted her remark.

"It's true," agreed another girl. "His nasty green eyes were seen looking in the class room window only minutes before she came in and caught Rosa and me playing naughts and crosses."

"Then I count we'll be caught tonight and sent home in disgrace," said Jane gloomily.

"Don't worry Jane," said Lizzie soothingly.

"Clement won't catch us, the mere hint of a cat near me and I start sneezing dreadfully. You'll have plenty of time to get back to bed before he can report us."

"Let's get on with the meeting," said a girl called Biddy impatiently.

"Hold hands everyone then," ordered Lizzie.

Just as they were about to raise their linked hands towards the centre of the circle, the candle flame, which had been burning steadily all along, made a sudden sputtering noise and flickered wildly. Long thin tongues of fire shot out from it in all directions, throwing grotesque shadows on the walls around them.

Jane wasn't the only one to gasp nervously. "What was that? What happened?" came in anguished whispers from around the little group.

"Just a draught," said Lizzie stoutly. "Come on, we'll just have to start again."

They held up their arms once more. Lizzie picked up the candlestick from the floor.

"What are we here for?" she intoned solemnly.

"To plan a dare," they all replied.

"What is our aim?"

"Friendship and fun."

"What is our name?"

"Banshees of St Brigid's."

"Now Rosa," Lizzie ordered "Pick out a dare."

Instantly Rosa produced from under her

3

voluminous cloak a tapestry bag, which she shook vigorously. Then she plunged her hand into it and drew out a rolled up spiral of paper.

Unrolling it carefully she leaned towards the light and announced dramatically: "The chosen *Banshee* has to break into Sr Bernard's study, where she will stand in the middle of the room and sing in a loud voice the school song, not stopping even if Bernard herself comes in and catches her. As proof of this daring feat, she will steal the day's date from the big calendar on the nun's desk. Remember that *Banshees* are on their honour to do the whole dare."

Jane shook her head. "I count that's too hard," she said soberly. "I'd be petrified to go into Sr Bernard's study. If I'm chosen, I'll definitely pay the fine and tell you a story instead."

"Let's hope you don't get chosen then," said Biddy in her frank way. "All your stories are so dull and gloomy."

"Banshees can do *any* dare," Lizzie hastily intervened. "Remember how pleased everyone was when we got that extra hour's sleep due to Rosa accepting the dare to change the school clock back an hour."

"It was great!" chuckled Sarah. "Especially when our so perfect class prefect, Emer, was nearly blamed for it."

"She would have been too, only she's so well in with Sr Bernard," said Anne.

4

"Maybe locking her in the wash-up room with Clement did the trick," said Rosa grimly.

"We should have locked them in different rooms," laughed Lizzie "Then he couldn't have supported her story. Anyway, it's choosing time now."

Rosa produced her bag again. This time she loosened the drawstrings and held it out to her neighbour.

"You start, Biddy," she said "then Sarah, Anne, Jane and then you Lizzie."

Biddy leant forward and, to her obvious relief, picked a blank. So each member dipped their hand in and tried their luck.

"I've got it! I got the black spot!" called Lizzie, not noticeably worried, holding up a small circle of black paper. "Now my problem is when will I do it?"

"I think the best time would be about half six in the evening," suggested Biddy. "It's the nuns supper time, and even Bernard has to eat."

"Good idea," agreed Sarah. "Or even seven o'clock. They are all usually at recreation then."

"That's study time," protested Lizzie. "I can't wander around the school when I'm meant to be with everyone in the hall."

"True enough," said Ann. "You'd be bound to meet someone who'd want to know what you were doing in the corridors at that time."

"I know what you can do," said Rosa excitedly. "I have music practice between half six and seven tomorrow. We can swap. Remember, you have to pass near the study to get to the music room."

"Well done, Rosa," said Lizzie gratefully. "I'll do that. It will be simple to leave the music room about a quarter to seven and do the dare then. Wish me luck, *Banshees*, especially while I'm singing the school song."

"You'll need it," said Jane, shaking her head dolefully as before.

"I'd give a lot to actually see you singing in Sr Bernard's study," chuckled Sarah.

"Don't forget to get your proof, or we won't believe you," laughed Rosa.

"I won't. I suppose the calendar is still on her desk," replied Lizzie.

"It is," said Sarah. "I had to go to Sr Bernard the other day to get permission to write to my cousin and I saw it then. It's on a big wooden stand with the date, the year and some wise saying written on the bottom of the page. You can't miss it."

"Great!" said Lizzie "It's time to make our oath of secrecy, then we'd better go back to bed."

"I agree," said Anne yawning. "I find it hard enough getting up at six am when I get to bed at the proper time, as it is."

Suddenly the candle flame flickered wildly as before, only this time it went out, leaving the stricken group in utter darkness. In the subsequent confusion, most of the *Banshees* got up, bumping into each other and tripping noisily over boxes in a mad scramble for the door.

Lizzie, however, kept her head and within seconds the welcome sound of a match being struck was heard, followed by the restoration of candle light once more.

"Look!" cried Rosa "The door is open, that's what must have caused the draught which put the candle out."

"That's odd," mused Lizzie as she led the way out of the room. "Surely whoever was last in must have closed the door."

No one could remember being last in. "I think we all came in together, just behind you," whispered Sarah as they reached their dormitory again.

2

Modern Times

About a hundred years later, on a crisp day in early autumn, when the combination of warm sun and fresh air had lured the whole school out to watch the first hockey match of the season, Judith O'Brien, only lately released from the infirmary after a bout of 'flu, stood looking disconsolately out of the common room window.

As she looked listlessly at the sun dancing on the river Boyne, which flowed serenely past the old castle, a burst of wild cheering came drifting across to her on the still air. Groaning, she banged the window shut and threw herself onto the battered couch, turning on the television as she did so. She was watching somewhat listlessly a parrot flapping its wings and shrieking *"Pieces of eight, pieces of eight"* from the shoulder of a one legged man on the deck of an old-fashioned sailing ship when the door of the room burst open behind her.

"Hi Judith," called a cheerful voice. "How are

you? I've only heard this minute that you were down again."

Judith, turning eagerly around, saw a girl smiling at her from the open doorway. "Nuala" she called joyfully "Am I glad to see you! How is the match going?"

Nuala came into the room and sat down beside her. "Fast and furious. There's no score yet, but I think we've a good chance of winning all the same."

"Brilliant!" said Judith, adding wistfully "I wish I could go out and watch it myself. Why are you in here anyway?"

"Oh, I had to take a message in for Miss Lawless," replied Nuala rather vaguely. Then, to Judith's surprise, she ran over and, carefully closing the common room door, leant against it.

"It has just occurred to me that everyone, just everyone is out watching the match," she said, her eyes sparkling. "Let's think of something interesting to do as we have the place to ourselves."

"What, for instance?" replied Judith, not particularly impressed by the idea.

"Well, let me see, let's go somewhere where none of us have gone before, for example," said Nuala "No, I've got it! What about this museum they're opening tomorrow? We can have a sneak preview of it for starters."

"A museum, that's news to me. What's it for?"

"It's in honour of our 150th anniversary. Remember – it's going to be a St Brigid's museum. I hear they've rooted out every ancient cup and shield and all the records going back to the day the school was opened, not to mention hundreds of photographs. They should be a good laugh anyway."

"I must have missed hearing about it while I was sick," replied Judith. "I do remember a lot of talk about the celebrations all right, some sort of party and maybe a concert was mentioned. Where is it?"

"The museum, you mean? The ground floor room of the east tower has been given over to it."

"Wait a minute, the east tower, that's where we sleep, isn't it?"

"Correct. We're on the third floor. I think some fifth or maybe sixth years are on the second floor. The top room is empty, I believe."

Due to a large increase in the number of pupils attending St Brigid's, the dormitories had been extended, with some of the rooms in the twin towers adjacent to them being pressed into service. Everyone wanted to sleep in one of the tower rooms, even though the cubicles in them were much smaller than any of the ones in the regular dormitories. Consequently, Nuala, Judith, Aileen and Josie along with Deirdre and Ciara, were thrilled when they were chosen to be the first occupants of the third floor room in the east tower.

10

Even though it was connected to St Anne's dormitory by an old oak door in its thick stone walls, they felt that Annie's pocket, as they called it, had a special atmosphere of its own. Nuala had summed it up as a kind of weird, even creepy feeling, not frightening, but different.

"Are you sure the museum is open?" Judith asked now.

"I am," replied Nuala. "Gobnait announced only this morning that although it wasn't quite finished, the museum would be open to all, to give us a chance to bone up on our splendid heritage."

Judith grinned appreciatively at this. "I can just hear her saying it," she said. "Anyway, it's a super idea to see it before the hordes crush in tomorrow."

"That's what I thought," agreed Nuala as she led the way out of the common room and along the corridor towards the stairs.

"Doesn't it make you feel a bit weird when you consider that for 150 years this old square castle with its twin towers has been a school to scores and scores of girls?" Nuala said thoughtfully as they were running lightly down the long staircase.

"It is a bit creepy when you come to think of it," replied Judith. "It's a wonder we've never had a haunting here."

Nuala laughed. "What a crazy thought. Girls have always been dying to get out of school, not get back in to it."

Once they had passed through the door connecting the castle to the east tower, they felt some of their confidence draining away. Maybe it was the strangely quiet atmosphere which gave the impression of waiting for someone or something. Even the sunlight shining in through the lancet windows was diffused and softened here, unlike the rest of the castle. Nuala opened the narrow oak door of the only room there and peeped in nervously. To her surprise, it was lined with modern glass cases and stands all stacked with silver cups and medals. The walls were covered with photographs of every size and description, some faded and yellow with age.

"Wow!" exclaimed Nuala. "What an eyeful!"

Judith, close behind her, was equally impressed. "Look at those uniforms. Long skirts almost to the ground with buttoned up bodices and long tight sleeves. How did they bear to wear such gear?"

Nuala made no reply, as she was engrossed in looking at the part of the wall which was covered with deep green, heart-shaped boards, each topped with twenty small silver shields. Each of these shields had a girl's name engraved on it, as well as the year it was presented to her.

"It's the name of the winners of the *Merry Gold Medal* going back about one hundred and twenty years," cried Nuala in an excited voice.

Judith went over to see for herself. "The *Merry Gold Medal*? what's that given for?" she asked.

"Once upon a time it was very big here, the whole school voted for the nicest girl in St Brigid's," explained Nuala. "Aileen swears her great-grandmother won it one year. Anyway, a few years ago the whole thing was changed and now it's only awarded to the girl who achieves something really special in sixth year. Don't you remember Maeve Murphy getting it last year for winning the best science fiction prize in the RDS?"

"Of course, I'd forgotten about her. Well, that's dished my chances of winning it. I might have managed the nicest girl in the school though," grinned Judith.

"Imagine the whole school sitting down and solemnly voting for the nicest girl there," mused Nuala. "Do you think everyone went around behaving like angels for a few days before the voting or did they just vote for their friends?"

"We'll never know now anyway," replied Judith. "Look, there's a shield with no name on it between the shields for 1895 and 1897."

"I wonder why?" said Nuala, looking with interest at the odd one out. "It must be 1896, exactly a hundred years ago this year. What a coincidence."

"Wow!" said Judith. "You're right. How strange."

"I'd love to know who she was," said Nuala. "And why her name isn't on it."

"Perhaps she lost her temper in front of the

13

whole school or something," replied Judith lightly, losing interest. She moved over to look at a group of curios including a piece of coral from the South Seas, if the label on it was correctly written.

When she turned to see what Nuala was doing, she was startled to find herself looking into the wrong end of a hollow pipe made of wood.

"Don't worry" said Nuala, looking up and seeing the expression on her face. "This is only the blow pipe, I haven't put the poisoned dart into it yet."

"Help!" cried Judith "Where did that come from?"

Nuala carefully placed a little dart into the blowpipe before replying. "According to a card lying there on that table, it was bequeathed to the school by one Bronagh Kelly, whose uncle was a missionary in Brazil."

Nuala carefully aimed the pipe and blew hard. She was greatly surprised when the little feathered dart flew out from the pipe and across the room where it embedded itself in the door, only seconds before it opened, admitting Miss Ryan into the room.

Nuala paled and cried out "Oh no! I never thought it would work, I really didn't!"

Judith ran over and plucked the dart out of the door and hid it behind her back. "Oh, hello Miss Ryan," she said quickly. "We're just having a look at the, er, museum. I am not allowed outside yet, you see."

"I'm glad to see you're better, Judith," replied

the teacher in a friendly voice, obviously not noticing Nuala's strange behavior. "How do you like the museum?"

"Oh, its brilliant, simply brilliant," said Judith enthusiastically. "Nuala, you must show Miss Ryan that shield that's missing its name." As she spoke, she waved the dart meaningfully behind her back.

"Of course, Judith," Nuala said recovering from her fright. She handed the blowpipe to Judith and then led the teacher over to where the *Merry Gold Medal* shields were on the wall, pointing out the blank one and asking questions about it. While the teacher was thus distracted, Judith quietly put the blowpipe and the dart back in their correct places before joining the others.

"We don't know the history of that one yet," Miss Ryan was explaining to Nuala. "As we haven't all the records sorted out yet. Don't worry, as soon as I know the story, I'll let you know its secret."

"Thank you, Miss Ryan," said Nuala gratefully. She couldn't explain why, even to herself, but the history of the blank shield interested her enormously.

"I wonder would you girls mind taking these books to the library for me?" asked the history teacher, taking two volumes out of her bag. "As Mrs Long is away at the moment, just leave them on her desk." Mrs Long was the extremely capable school librarian.

15

As they were leaving the museum, Miss Ryan called over to them. "I've just remembered some of the sixth years are looking after the library today."

Once the door was safely closed behind them, Nuala sighed deeply and said "Gosh, that was a lucky miss, wasn't it? If she had come into the room even a minute earlier, she might have got that dart in her face. I haven't got over the shock of it yet."

Judith nodded in agreement. "Especially as it might have been one with some deadly poison on it; you could have ended up on a murder charge," she pointed out ghoulishly.

3

The Old Library

Though the school library was housed in one of the big rooms at the front of the castle, there was nothing old fashioned about it. Decorated in a combination of pale pine and smooth plastics, it was very modern and functional. Mrs Long, the dedicated and efficient librarian, complete with her computer, liked it that way. The girls had no complaints either, in fact they were very proud of it.

Arriving in due course at the library, Nuala and Judith were surprised to find it completely empty. Dim and shadowy in the failing light, it was so quiet that the two friends were acutely conscious of their footsteps echoing loudly on the polished floor as they crossed over to the librarian's desk.

"You really miss Mrs Long bustling about the place, don't you?" whispered Judith. "The library seems odd without her."

"Well, I'm glad she isn't here, she gives me the

creeps," said Nuala. "Those all-seeing eyes watching your every move."

"She does watch us very closely," Judith conceded. "I wonder why, what does she think we'll do in here?"

"Eat the books probably," said Nuala. "She always makes me think of a witch with those big green eyes and that purring voice always asking questions."

Judith had to laugh. "You make her sound more like the witch's cat than the witch," she commented.

"I bet she's a mixture of both," replied Nuala briskly.

A loud creaking noise which seemed to come from a set of large bookcases halfway down the room made them both jump.

"Let's get out of here, I'm scared!" said Judith, but Nuala was made of sterner stuff.

Pushing Judith gently aside, she walked very quietly down the room and peered between the bookcases in question. Judith heard her mutter:

"Gosh, I never knew that there was one here before," then she seemed to disappear.

"Nuala, Nuala!" called Judith as a horrible cold feeling came over her. She hurried down the room to where Nuala had vanished. When she got there she was amazed to see an open door in the wall between two big bookcases. Though very frightened, she immediately walked through the door and into another room. The first thing that struck her was the smell; a mixture of leather, old books and dust.

"Nuala," she whispered loudly. Instantly it seemed Nuala was beside her, her eyes shining with excitement.

"Isn't this cool!" she said. "It's my idea of a real library. Just look at the books! There's simply thousands of them."

Judith's eyes widened as she took in the details of the place. Big mahogany book shelves with funny shaped tops, leather armchairs, lots of round tables and even a large globe of the world at one end of the room. This was nothing compared to the books. Thousands of them filled every available space; shelves were crammed full with them, they spilled over tables and chairs and lay in heaps on the floor.

"Hello girls, can I help you?" asked a cheerful voice. They looked up and saw a tall thin girl in front of them.

"Th . . . this place," stammered Nuala. "Where did it come from?"

The newcomer laughed merrily, an infectious sound. "It's always been here as far as I know," she replied "It's the original library of the castle."

"That explains it!" said Nuala to Judith. "They must keep it locked up."

"Well," said the strange girl "It's not usually open to the school, but as you are here I must give you a book to read."

Turning, she picked up quite a large volume bound in dark brown with gold lettering on it.

"Before I give it to you, will you promise to read it?" asked the girl earnestly.

Nuala was torn in two. On the one hand she didn't like refusing such a friendly person, on the other she didn't want to promise something she mightn't be able to keep.

Judith nudged her and whispered: "Promise her, I'll give you a hand with it."

So Nuala duly promised and the book was handed over. The girl then escorted them to the door, saying goodbye in the same friendly way as she had greeted them. As they left they could hear the door close softly behind them. Feeling slightly bemused they passed through the school library and walked down the stairs and over towards the common room again.

Judith broke the silence as they neared the common room. "I wonder who she was? She seemed very nice."

"I've been thinking about that," said Nuala. " She must be one of the new sixth years, there's a whole lot of new ones this term. I agree she is very nice, if a bit cracked. I wonder what her name is?"

Nuala squinted at the lettering on the brown book, then stopped dead in her tracks. "Judith!" she cried. "What have you made me promise? This book is written in a foreign language. It looks like Latin to me, but that's no help, I don't know Latin. I'll never be able to read it. What a trick to play on us!"

Judith took the book from her. She looked at the bold gold lettering and read out in a hesitant voice: "*Alter Ipse Amicus.* I wonder what it means. I'll give you a hand with it when we get back to the common room. That girl seemed really anxious that we should read it."

"I know," agreed Nuala. "I did tell you she was cracked. Nice, but definitely potty."

When they reached the common room again all thought of trying to read the book was driven from their minds as the room was full of laughing, chattering girls. St Brigid's had beaten Glenmara by six goals to three in the hockey match. Nuala and Judith were so interested in hearing all about the match that Nuala flung the book into her locker and promptly forgot all about it.

Everyone had to welcome Judith back into their midst again and tell her how much they all had missed her.

"Not that you missed anything while you were sick," said Eithne. "Just the same old dull round of lessons. In history: the famine, in geography: the woman's place in industry, and lots of learning of lines from *Romeo and Juliet*."

This made everyone laugh.

"Eithne, you make it sound so enticing, I just can't wait to get back," Judith said wryly.

"That reminds me," said Josie, "Sr Patrick is waiting for you to come back before we start work on our puppets."

"Great!" said Judith happily. "I just love working with clay. I think I'll make mine a race horse."

"Don't forget the 150th celebrations," said Grainne. "Miss Ryan says that one of the teachers has written a pageant which will be staged showing the highlights of the school during the 150 years. It might be fun to see."

"Then there's the special free day," said Nuala.

"What's special about it?" asked Aileen.

"Well, it's supposed to be a day which we will celebrate exactly as they did years ago, before half terms were thought of."

"Great stuff!" said Aileen. "I've often heard that in the past free days were super. A late sleep, terrific food and a special game of hide and seek in the dark were some of the things mentioned."

"They're going to have a Past/Present hockey match too," said Eithne.

"Would any past pupil bother coming back?" asked Grainne skeptically.

"Of course, they love coming back, dressing up

in track suits, playing hockey and talking about their happy days in St Brigid's," said Fidelma. " And all the great crack they had here."

"You'll be as bad yourself," said Nuala. "Anyway, it certainly looks as if we won't be bored this term."

"There's the bell for supper, thank goodness," said Fidelma, jumping up and making for the door. "Coming, Twin?"

"Yes indeed," said Eithne. "Watching hockey matches and gossiping always makes me ravenously hungry!"

"I didn't think you needed anything to make you hungry," laughed Judith as she followed her cousins out of the room.

"For that I will visit you in your famous tower room tonight and I will expect a conducted tour," threatened Eithne.

"I'm coming too," giggled Fidelma.

"Well, if you want to risk the trouble of leaving your dorm, I'll show you our tower room. There's nothing I like better than giving conducted tours of it," replied Judith sarcastically, not believing the twins had meant it seriously.

Later that night, as Judith was talking to Nuala outside her cubicle she was surprised to see the handle of the door in Annie's Pocket turn slowly. As she watched, the door opened just enough to let her cousins Eithne and Fidelma slip in.

23

"Hi Judith, we've come for the tour," said Eithne boldly.

"Get on with it too, it's nearly lights out time," said Fidelma cheekily.

Judith looked from one identical face to the other. "You're the goofiest pair in the school," she said crossly. "What are you up to? You must have seen this room dozens of times before this."

"We haven't," said Eithne. "We were waiting for you to get better before we visited, but if it's too much trouble, we'll leave, won't we, Fidelma?"

"Absolutely, we always know when we're not wanted," agreed Fidelma.

"Come on, then," said Judith. She took them into the centre of the room.

"This is the third floor room of the east tower," she rattled off. "As you can see, it has six cubicles, crushed and crowded into this tiny space. An ancient square window looks out on the River Boyne, one of Ireland's most prestigious rivers."

"She does it well, doesn't she?" said Eithne as Judith paused for breath.

"Yes, we'll have to give her a generous tip," agreed Fidelma.

Judith, ignoring her tormentors, prattled on. "That door you see in the back wall leads up a stone staircase to the top room of the tower which is unoccupied – as far as we know."

"Why don't you take us up by this interesting

stone staircase so that we can see it for ourselves?" teased Eithne.

Judith, looking murderous, hissed through her teeth, "I can't for the simple reason that it's locked all the time."

"Pity," said Eithne. "But if it's locked there must be a key. It never worried us before – taking keys from the office."

Nuala, taking pity on Judith, explained "If you two nuisances look at the wall beside the door you can't miss seeing a square, sealed glass box with the key in it. Written on the box are instructions how to get the key out, but only in an emergency."

The two Murrays went over and examined the box.

"You know, Fidelma, I can see why this lot were picked to sleep in here," said Eithne.

"I can too," agreed Fidelma. "Imagine letting a little thing like a glass box come between you and getting that door open."

"Well, as it happens, we don't want it open," said Nuala.

"You might if you knew what we know," said Eithne. "Will we tell them about the lovely fire escape outside the window of the top room in the tower, leading all the way to the ground?"

"I don't believe you," said Aileen, who had now joined the party. "Anyway, they say that key is wired to an alarm bell that goes off in the office, where it summons the fire brigade."

"Good idea too," said Judith. "Can't you imagine what a temptation the fire escape would be to those fifth years in the room below us?"

"Not to mention us in this room too," grinned Nuala. "I'm sure we could find it very useful at times."

The lights out bell could be heard ringing, so Nuala and Judith urged their visitors to leave. Just as Eithne was about to pass through the door into the dormitory, she whispered to Nuala:

"They're not fifth years below you, they're sixth years, including two of the new girls. The rumor is that one of them was asked to leave her old school. She is a bit of a trickster I hear, though very pleasant."

The next minute she was gone.

"That book," declared Nuala and Judith simultaneously.

"I left it in my locker in the common room," said Nuala. "We must get it back tomorrow to the library. I hope Mrs Long doesn't devour me."

"A trickster," Eithne said.

"Though pleasant . . . " said Judith. "She certainly took us in. I thought she seemed genuinely nice."

"So did I," said Nuala "We'd better go to bed. First chance I have tomorrow I'll leave it back. Good night, Judith."

"'Night Nuala," said Judith flitting over to her own cubicle, reaching it just as the dormitory prefect came into check that everyone was in bed.

4

Alter Ipse Amicus

On the following afternoon while the rest of the class went off to the art room to work in clay Nuala, who didn't do art, gathered up her books, including the brown one with the gold lettering which she had retrieved earlier from her locker in the common room.

As she was leaving the classroom on her way to the hall to study, she nearly bumped into a panting Judith who was running towards her.

"Have you still got that book?" she enquired anxiously.

Nuala nodded in reply.

"Don't tell anyone about it, just meet me after school, usual place. I must fly."

Nuala nodded again, wondering what Judith was up to. She had rushed off in the direction of the art room again, so Nuala went down to the hall to study. There were about a dozen girls messing around and chatting there. When Sr Joan arrived soon afterwards everyone settled down to study.

Nuala hurried through her Maths and Irish. Then she felt free to look at the strange brown book with its gold lettering. She placed it in front of her and read once again *Alter Ipse Amicus,* wishing she knew what these words meant. She tried to lift up the cover, but to her surprise the cover wouldn't budge. She examined it more carefully and discovered two tiny golden clasps were holding it down, which she swiftly undid. Now the book opened easily, but what a surprise awaited Nuala.

During the remainder of the study period Sr Joan looked down at Nuala several times and was greatly impressed by her close concentration on her work, mentally noting her as a very good student.

Eventually it was time to go. Nuala was out of the room like a shot, dumping her text books in the classroom before hurrying out to her and Judith's favourite meeting place. Very soon she was sitting in Barney, their special beech tree, impatiently waiting for Judith to appear. She hadn't long to wait. Judith didn't come alone either, she brought Aileen and Josie with her.

"You don't mind, do you?" she said as soon as the newcomers were sitting comfortably in their usual places. "I just thought they might be a help."

To Judith's surprise, Nuala only laughed at this remark. "Of course I don't mind," she said. "In fact,

I wouldn't dream of keeping a secret from my good friends. As our brown book says: *Alter Ipse Amicus*, meaning 'A Friend is Another Self'."

"Nuala, you genius! You've worked it out!" said Judith admiringly.

Nuala took the book out of a bag beside her. "Now look carefully," she said. "Here we have a book. Now I unclip these little clasps and behold, we have a book *within* a book."

"Wow!" said Josie. "That's brilliant."

Nuala took the second book from where it lay snugly in its special box. "This," she said "Is a very special book. A hundred years ago exactly, in this school, a small group of girls got together and formed a society for friendship and fun. This is the diary of the *Banshees of St Brigid's*. What do you think of that?"

"Good stuff," said Aileen. "Let's hear more about this society. For instance, what did they do?"

"Well, they were a secret society which met at night when everyone was in bed asleep. You'll never guess where they met though," said Nuala, who was in great spirits.

"I bet it was here in Barney," said Judith. "The tree is definitely old enough."

"I agree, but its not the right answer."

"Go on Nuala, tell us," urged Josie. "You know we'll never guess it."

"In the top room of the tower, just above our

room," said Nuala. "They wore special clothes and masks and went up always after lights out. Imagine, all they had to light their way up there with was a candle."

"Wow!" said Josie. "I wouldn't care to go up those stone stairs with just a candle, it would be scary enough with a torch."

"What did they do there?" asked Aileen.

"I haven't finished reading the diary," said Nuala. "As you can see, it's in tiny handwriting, a bit faded in places too. But one thing I did discover was that they had a system of dares which one, and sometimes two members had to take on. If they failed or refused to do the dare, they were fined."

Nuala handed the book to Aileen, warning her to be careful with it. Aileen turned over the yellowing pages of the diary gently, as they seemed to be very brittle, before passing it on in turn to Judith and Josie.

"It's amazing, isn't it?" said Judith. "It's a bit creepy too, reading about real girls who actually were at school here a hundred years ago."

"It makes you think all right," said Josie as she handed the book back to Nuala. "I wonder did they ever sit in Barney just as we do? For all we know the tree could be haunted!"

"Good stuff," said Aileen. "I'd love to see one of the *Banshees* sitting here, maybe swapping tales of school life with us."

30

"No, no!" shouted Josie. "Don't Aileen, I'm scared of ghosts!"

"Don't be silly, Josie," said Nuala. "You're not interesting enough for a ghost to bother with you."

"Well, I like that!" said Josie, insulted.

"Does it give their names?" asked Judith, changing the subject.

"There are six names," said Nuala. "But all I can make out are Rosa something, Brigid Deegan, Jane T, and Liz Bruder." She closed the book and looked at them. "Do you realise that the one called Rosa turned the school clock back an hour one night and the whole school got an extra hour's sleep in consequence!"

"Great stuff," said Aileen. "I bet that was a popular one. Any more dares, Nuala?"

"As it's the centenary of the Banshee club, what would you think of reopening it again ourselves? I think it could be great fun," she said.

"Why not?" said Aileen. "We could do the same dares but in a modern way. For instance, using the intercom. Nuala, you're a great mimic, you could pretend to be Sr Gobnait and give a message to the school over it."

"I don't think it would be that easy," laughed Nuala. "But Aileen, you've got the right idea."

Josie tossed her long hair back. "I'm with you too, Nuala. What sort of costumes did they wear?" she asked.

"Long grey cloaks and masks, I gather," said Nuala. "I don't know about the cloaks, but Halloween masks would be easy enough to acquire."

"The shops are full of them at present," agreed Aileen. "What about you, Judith?"

"Of course, do you think I'd hold back? I think those grey cloaks were their school ones, you know how keen they were on cloaks years ago. The only idea I could suggest would be sheets, or maybe quilt covers with a hole in them."

"Great idea Ju, we could slip our heads through the hole, but what about our arms?" said Aileen enthusiastically.

"Not to mention our mothers," said Nuala. "I know mine would have a fit if she found holes in my covers."

"I know!" said Aileen excitedly. "You know those jumbo plastic refuse sacks, they come in green and black? We could cut holes in them and pull them over our heads and cut holes for the arms too."

"Good idea, Aileen," said Nuala. "But isn't plastic supposed to be dangerous over your head?"

"Not as long as we pin the plastic to our collars; it won't go over our faces," said Aileen impatiently.

"Don't be such a fuss-pot Nuala. I think we should get those huge green sacks because they rustle crisply."

"But then everyone will hear us coming and going," protested Josie.

"That's the point!" said Aileen excitedly. "Can't you imagine the effect we would have on everyone? An ugly masked, green plastic ghost rustling around the dorms, we could terrorise the school!"

"I'm surprised at you Aileen," laughed Judith. "The *Banshees* is meant to be a club for friendship and fun."

"So what?" retorted Aileen. "We're the friends having a bit of fun."

"How did you work out the Latin bit?" asked Judith amidst the laughter which Aileen's remark had produced.

"Oh, that's explained in the diary," said Nuala. "They took it as their motto."

"We should have it printed on nice white cards then," said Aileen. "And whenever we carry out a dare we can leave one behind to let the school know who did it, like *Zorro*, or *The Shadow*."

"You're full of brilliant ideas today Aileen," said Josie admiringly.

"Thank you, Josie. I suppose it could have been the luscious dinner I had today that inspired me," replied Aileen grinning.

"How could you remind us of that awful cottage pie we had!" said Judith. "You know how much we hate it."

"How many of us will be in the club?" asked Josie. "And how will we keep it a secret?"

33

"That's a problem. I'd like to have all our friends in it," said Nuala. "But some of them are awful talkers."

"We'll just have to be extra careful who we take," said Josie. "You know what Gwendoline, and especially Monica, are like."

"I think we should recruit people in such a way that they won't know who we are," said Nuala. "I shall put an ad on the notice board in the common room for a start."

"What! You must be joking!" said Josie.

"No, I'm not, don't worry, I know what I'm doing. I suppose we could be masked too, during every meeting, I mean," said Nuala.

Josie looked at her watch. "I'll have to go now. There's a special hockey practice on this evening. I suppose we'll have to have another meeting ourselves before we really start. By the way, must we hold the *Banshee* meetings in the top room of the tower? There's no way we can get up to that place."

"That will have to be dealt with first," replied Nuala, looking determined. "Anyway, Josie, you go on, there's no point in incurring the wrath of the hockey captain by being late."

Josie grinned and slid down the tree.

"It's getting kind of chilly anyway," said Aileen. "I think we should go in and join the others in the common room."

"I agree," said Judith. "Not that there'll be anything on TV worth watching. It's so unfair that *Why Cases* are only shown at ten pm so that we never get a chance of seeing them."

"The sixth years are so lucky," said Aileen enviously. "They can video them and watch them the next day."

"Gwendoline says that the next episode is going to be really scary, all about an outbreak in a school, where strange phenomena appear in the corridors."

Why Cases, a programme where two agents investigate curious paranormal incidents which take place all over the world, had become a cult in St Brigid's, superseding *Together and Apart*, the one time prime favorite. The big disadvantage of the former was that it was only on TV when all the boarders were in bed. Sr Gobnait had had the foresight to have all the common rooms locked by nine-thirty each night, circumventing any daring girls who might have planned to sneak down and view it after lights out.

"I never thought Gobnait could be so mean not to let us see *Why Cases* just now and again." said Judith.

"Fat chance," laughed Aileen. "That's one of the reasons all these new girls are coming to the school: Mums and Dads want them to study hard and go to bed early. Aren't I right Nuala?"

Nuala nodded in agreement, but her mind was

35

on other things as she followed Aileen and Judith down the tree.

She was thinking deeply about the *Banshees* costume, remembering a book she had read once where it stated that banshees were originally just pretty fairies with long fair hair. Somehow Aileen's idea of a hideous mask topping a green plastic sack didn't quite fit in with that at all. She would have to come up with a better idea herself.

It was when they were walking towards the stairs which led to the common room floor that Nuala again saw the girl who had given her the book in the library. Before she had time to speak to her, the girl, giving Nuala a friendly smile, waved her hand and vanished through a door which led to the concert hall, where the stage was.

"That's it!" Nuala said to herself. "The props room is simply full of wigs and costumes. I must go there one day, and lift a few suitable things for the *Banshees*."

5

Spirit of St Brigid's

"What are you two whispering about?" asked Ciara, coming into the common room a few days later, just behind Josie and Deirdre, who were deep in conversation.

"Hi Ciara," said Josie, turning around. "We're not whispering, just talking about this pageant that has been inflicted on us."

On the previous night Sr Gobnait had held a meeting for the whole school at which she had announced the details of the forthcoming pageant, *Spirit of St Brigid's*. A portrayal of the school's history in drama, dance and song, was how she had described it. In fact, it was a sequence of scenes depicting highlights in the history of the school starting with the arrivals of the first nuns and pupils. These scenes were to be linked by short musical episodes giving some historical background about the area. Weaving its way through like a river was a dance which was already being called *Boyne Dance* by the girls.

"According to Eithne," said Deirdre, "that new girl in sixth year, you know, the very tall one with black hair, is a brilliant dancer. She has won prizes at *Feiseanna* all over the country. Anyway, she has been picked to be the lead in *Boyne Dance*."

"Wow!" said Ciara. "She must be good. I think the pageant sounds brilliant, I hope I get a part in it."

"You probably will," said Josie. "We all will unfortunately. I'm really worried about our free time, especially games time being taken up with rehearsals."

"I suppose Nuala will have a singing part. Lucky thing, I wish I could sing," said Ciara enviously, plainly taken up with the pageant, unlike Josie, who considered it a nuisance likely to interfere with more important interests.

"I'm sure she will," she replied in disgust. "And Aileen will probably be playing the violin and Judith painting scenery, and they'll be forever rushing off to rehearsals. I can see it's going to ruin any fun we might have this term."

As it happened, the three girls in question were at that moment in their tower bedroom concentrating on matters quite unrelated to the pageant.

Nuala was standing on a chair, stretching uncomfortably up trying to unscrew the glass box which contained the tower room key from the wall.

"It's too high up," she complained crossly. "If we had a fire it could be quite difficult to break it. I've a good mind to complain to Gobnait about it."

Aileen, who was holding the torch, chuckled. "Better wait until we've the key back in its box," she said.

"Steady with the light, Aileen!" complained Nuala. "It's wavering all over the place and I can't see what I'm doing. This screwdriver is much too light for the job as it is."

"It was the best I could get in the circs," said Aileen. "Remember, I was the one who found out that there was no connection between the box and the fire alarm, after a lot of skilful questioning at science class."

"Beam the light more to the left," commanded Nuala, not paying any attention to her.

In the silence that followed, Judith peered anxiously at them from the dormitory door where she stood as lookout.

There was a sound like something scratching and scraping against the wall and Nuala announced triumphantly, if somewhat inaudibly due to the screws clenched between her teeth, "Got it!"

Judith could see the glass box hanging precariously from the one corner which was still attached to the wall.

Nuala untaped the key from the wall, then dropped it down to Aileen, who missed it. It fell with a thud on the floor. Aileen groped frantically around but couldn't find it in the dark.

"Leave it, Aileen, I need the light," said Nuala, taping a substitute key on the wall and swiftly screwing the box back into position.

"Switch off the torch," hissed Judith from the door. "There's someone moving around in the dorm outside."

She held the door open a crack and peered out. To her horror the person was walking towards their room. Closing the door gently, she turned to where the other two were standing frozen in position.

"Quick, get out of sight!" she whispered urgently. "They're coming this way."

Nuala grabbed the chair, diving into her cubicle. She slipped under her bed, pulling the quilt down over the side of it. Aileen and Judith followed suit.

The door of the room opened gently and someone came in very quietly. As the light wasn't switched on, Nuala risked peering out from under her bed. All she was able to catch sight of were a pair of thin legs and a portion of uniform skirt.

Judging by the rattling sounds, they guessed that their visitor was messing with the locked door which opened on to the stone staircase in the tower.

It seemed hours to the three hiding under their beds, but it wasn't much more than seven or eight minutes later that the mysterious intruder left the room as quietly as she had come in.

"What was all that about, I wonder?" said Judith, as the three of them crawled out from under their beds. "Did either of you see anything?"

"I did," said Nuala, briskly brushing herself down. "Even though all I did see was legs and half a uniform skirt, it was definitely one of the school, and judging by the legs I think it was either a fifth or sixth year."

Aileen shone her torch over to the locked door. "She was messing with the door anyway," she said. "I wonder why? Maybe she found the key on the floor somewhere."

"It didn't sound like a key in a lock to me," said Judith, going over to the door and shining her torch around the floor there. "Aha! I see it!" she cried, running over to the back of a cubicle and picking something up from the ground there.

"It's a complete mystery," said Nuala. "But thank goodness we've got the key. I must hide it somewhere safe in my cube. Lend me your torch, Ju."

She reappeared quite soon. Looking satisfied, she handed the torch back to Judith, who said:

"It's getting late, Nuala. I think we should get out of here fast, you never know who might come up and catch us."

So they left their room, passing swiftly and silently through the dormitory and downstairs to the common room.

As they were walking along, Aileen asked Nuala could she remember anything else about the intruder. Nuala thought for a moment, then she said,

"She was wearing runners, when I come to think of it. They seemed to have a red light on the heels which flashed on and off as she walked."

"I know the sort," said Aileen. "I didn't know anyone in the school had them though."

"Then they should be easy enough to trace," said Judith. "We'll just have to keep a watch out on all the fifth and sixth years' feet."

As they were turning in the common room door, Nuala said in a low voice to her two companions, "I think we should only tell Josie about our strange experience."

To their surprise, the common room was almost empty. On enquiry, they discovered that the list of people chosen to take part in the pageant had just been put up on the notice board outside Sr Gobnait's office, and everyone had gone off to find out who was on it, so they went down to join them. Needless to say, there was a large, rather noisy crowd standing around the notice board, all eager to read the lists. As they approached, Josie came way from it. Spying Aileen, she hurried over.

"Hi Aileen, where have you been? Don't bother going over there. I'll tell you all about it."

Judith and Nuala joined them then.

"As I expected, Nuala, you have a singing part. Most of the important parts have gone to fifth and some sixth years. Nearly everyone will be dragged into the crowd scenes," said Josie, adding with satisfaction "Rehearsals will be mostly in the morning and during class hours, and that'll only be for the principals for the first few weeks."

"I knew about my part," said Nuala "But did you notice who the dancing team was? There's a rumour going round that the new black-haired girl in sixth year, Eilís something or other, is a brilliant dancer."

"I heard that too," said Josie. "She is the leader of the dance team, so it looks as if the story is true."

"I thought that there were two new girls in sixth year with black hair," said Judith. "Which one is Eilís?"

"Ciara says that the very tall one is Eilís, the other girl is quite different looking. She has a very pale, long, saintly looking face and wears her hair parted in the middle. Her name is Clementine – of all things," said Josie.

"I know her now," said Judith "At least I heard that she is the one who had to leave her last school in a hurry. Eithne's aunt apparently heard the whole story in the hairdressers, but refused to give her the details."

"Trust Eithne," laughed Aileen. "She'll find out yet. I'd back her anytime."

Nuala looked at Judith. "I wonder is she the one we met in the library? Her hair was long and black and she had a very pale face," she said.

Judith looked thoughtful. "I suppose so, but she had a lovely smile too," she said at last.

"True enough," said Nuala "*Alter Ipse Amicus* has turned out to be very interesting too, hasn't it?"

Judith laughed "It has indeed."

The subject of their talk, Eilís and Clementine, happened to be at that moment in the latter's cubicle in the tower bedroom above the heritage museum. Sixth years usually had single bedrooms, but this term, due to so many new girls, the tower room had been pressed into service. In consideration of their seniority, only four girls shared this room, unlike six in the other rooms.

"I got the job done as arranged, Clem," said one of the girls. "I had no trouble at all."

"Good," said Clem, taking a long black garment from the back of her wardrobe and draping it carefully around herself.

"What do you think, Eilís?" she asked, combing her straight black hair so that it fell curtain-like on either side of her pale face.

Eilís looked with admiration at the black cloak covered with signs of the zodiac picked out in silver on it which the other girl was wearing. "It's cool, really cool," she said enthusiastically. "Have you any other Wiccan things?"

Clementine's pale face showed no animation as she answered egnimatically, "That depends . . . "

Suddenly there were four loud knocks on the door of the room. Eilís ran over and unlocked it, admitting two girls who came in all excitement.

"Wow, Clem, you look brilliant! Doesn't she, June?" said one of the newcomers.

"Brilliant Kelly, just brilliant," replied the other newcomer. "Turn around Clem, let's see it really properly."

Clem solemnly revolved around in front of her friends.

"Do you wear anything on your head?" asked June.

Clem shook her head slowly.

"What did you mean by saying *'Depends'?* asked Eilís suddenly. "Depends on what?"

"On whether you three can be trusted," replied Clem.

"Of course we can be trusted," said Eilís indignantly. "Why do you say that?"

"I thought that once about other people, and they babbled, and it led to trouble," replied Clem, taking off her cloak and carefully putting it away in a special box in her wardrobe.

"We're not like that," said Eilís quickly. "We'll promise not to tell any secrets to anyone, won't we?" she appealed to the other two.

"Will you solemnly swear not to reveal to

anyone, no matter who, whatever I tell you about the *Craft*?" Clem asked, looking piercingly at each of them in turn.

"Happily," said Eilís immediately. "What about you two?"

"Not to anybody, ever?" asked Kelly.

"Well, until I give you leave," replied Clem calmly. "I'm not really allowed to tell people about the *Craft*, unless they are prepared to swear to secrecy. It's a professional thing."

"Like doctors and lawyers, you mean?" said June. "Well, if it's like that, I'll swear."

"So will I," said Kelly.

Clementine stretched out her hands towards them. "Lay your hands on mine," she ordered "And repeat after me: I solemnly swear never to reveal any Wiccan secrets that I have learned from Clementine, under any circumstances whatsoever."

Just as they were about to repeat their promise, Clem stopped them. "I just want you to know that you'd better really mean this promise, or something dreadful may happen," she warned grimly.

Feeling nervous, but excited, the three girls repeated after Clem their promise of secrecy.

Just as they said the last words, the lights in their room flickered and went out, leaving them in total darkness.

No one was more surprised at this unexpected turn of events than Clementine herself. Naturally, she didn't mention this to her companions when they gasped in fright.

"I really meant that promise," June's voice wavered in the dark.

"So did I," replied Eilís and Kelly simultaneously.

"Then you've nothing to fear," said Clem more calmly than she felt.

6

The Return of The Banshees

Despite all the excitement of the pageant, not to mention the usual routine of class and study, Nuala hadn't forgotten about the recruitment of extra members to the *Banshee* club. She had discussed this with Judith, Josie and Aileen and they had all agreed that the other two members of Annie's Pocket, plus Judith's cousins, the Murrays, should be given first refusal, as it were.

In consequence, the four girls in question were intrigued one morning to find four envelopes inside each of their lockers, marked *Top Secret* and addressed to them in an unfamiliar hand. Each of these envelopes contained the following invitation:

Are you bored, depressed, looking for excitement or merely enjoy friendship and fun? Here is the answer – A group dedicated to improving the quality of not only our lives, but the lives of our fellow guests in St Brigid's.

If you are interested, write your name on the back of this form and drop it in the Mission box outside Sr Gobnait's office before 6 pm this evening.

FAINT HEARTS ARE NOT WELCOME!

The Murrays enthusiastically signed their names and dropped their note unobtrusively into the mission box as they passed it on their way to class. Deirde acted similarly, but Ciara was slower to sign her name. It wasn't that she didn't like fun, but the *Faint hearts* bit was a bit worrying. In the end sheer curiosity got the better of her and she duly posted her note too.

Nuala, who had her contacts, in this particular case Lorraine Pals who was treasurer of the Mission Society, duly passed the signed note over to her before dinner time.

During dinner, Judith asked Eithne, who was sitting beside her, would she and Fidelma come out to Barney after the meal as she had something important to tell them. Eithne, thinking it was family news, looked out the window and replied,

"I can spare you about fifteen minutes as I have promised to go with Fidelma and practise basketball with a few of the team."

"Fine," replied Judith. "I'll see you then."

On the way out of the refectory, Aileen managed to contact Deirdre with the same request, and Josie did likewise with Ciara.

When they arrived at the giant beech tree, Nuala was already there waiting to greet them. "Hi gang," she said. "I suppose you've guessed by now that it was me who sent you the invites."

"We should have known," said Fidelma. "What an idiot you are Nuala, why didn't you ask us directly?"

Nuala looked pained. "Have you no discretion Fidelma? I wanted to make sure that you were prepared to co-operate before I told you the details," she said.

"What would you have done if we hadn't?" asked Deirdre.

"There are others who would have jumped at the chance of joining our exclusive society," said Nuala grinning at them. "You don't know how privileged you are."

"Do you want to join or not?" asked Josie impatiently. "If you do, Nuala will tell you all about it. If not, you can go."

"Keep your hair on, young Cleary," said Eithne. "We never said we wouldn't join, but it better be good."

"Do you want to hear the details, Deirdre?" Aileen asked. "You too Ciara?"

They both nodded, so Nuala told them the whole story and about the idea of reviving *Banshees of St Brigid's*.

"Cool, cool," breathed Deirdre. "I think it's just brilliant the way you told it."

"Good stuff," said Aileen. "That's the reaction we all like to hear."

"When's the first meeting and what will we do

for gear?" asked Eithne, forgetting all about her plans for basketball practice.

"That's a bit of a problem, but I have some ideas which I hope to put into execution tomorrow," replied Nuala.

"Why tomorrow?" asked Aileen.

"Because tomorrow we will be having the first practice for this pageant," explained Nuala "And it just occurred to me that it will give me a chance to get near some costumes and wigs. You never know, I might find something suitable."

"What about Aileen's plastic sacks?" asked Josie.

"Well," said Nuala tactfully, "I think they are marvellous, but I just read lately that banshees originally were beautiful fairy women with long flowing hair, who drove men mad with their beauty. Somehow I just don't feel that green plastic sacks would be correct in the circumstances."

"What men will we meet to drive mad with our beauty?" asked Aileen in surprise.

"None," replied Nuala succinctly. "It's a nice idea though. Don't cancel the sacks Aileen, we'll need them to hide our gear in."

"I suppose it will be a few days before we can have our first meeting," said Ciara.

"It will give us all time to think up some really terrific dares," said Judith.

"Another thing, don't forget to look out for sixth years with light strips on the heels of their runners," warned Nuala. "I'd like to know why we had that mysterious visitor in our room."

"How will you manage about meetings?" Deirdre asked the twins. "It'll be easy for us, we're all together in one room, but you two will be out in the dorm, remember."

"Leave that to us," said Fidelma. "We'll manage."

"Just let us know the time and the place and we'll turn up. I must get a new battery for my torch. I suppose we'll be using torches, Nuala, not candles."

"Definitely not candles," said Nuala. "Much too dangerous."

"Talking about time," said Eithne "We must fly. Let us know about the gear as soon as you can, Nuala. Come on, Fidelma."

The Murrays hurried off, followed in a more leisurely manner by the rest of the *Banshees*.

Physics was the first class of the afternoon. As they sat down in their places, Miss Crilly announced:

"We have been studying light and how it travels in a straight line. Today I want to demonstrate dispersion. As you can see, I am placing this card, which has a slit in it, in front of the projector, as I want to produce a narrow beam of light."

Arranging a transparent glass block with triangular ends and rectangular sides between the

projector and a screen in front of her, she asked
Monica, "What is this object called?"

"A prism, Miss Crilly."

"Very good, Monica. Now, everyone, watch and
note what happens when I beam the white light
through this prism."

A chorus of exclamations arose from the class
when a band of colors, red, orange, yellow, green,
blue, indigo and violet appeared upon the screen.

"This shows that white light is made up of
different colours," the teacher pointed out. "It is
caused by the fact that the different colours which
make up white light travel at different speeds in the
glass prism. Can any of you suggest some well
known natural occurrence which is caused by the
same principle?"

"Could it be a rainbow?" asked Josie.

"Quite right. Rainbows are formed when
sunlight is dispersed by rain droplets in the
atmosphere."

It occurred to Judith, who had been watching
the experiment with great interest, that it could
have possibilities for a *Banshee* dare. For instance,
what reaction would she get if she covered her
torch with a card that had a narrow slit in it, then
shone it through a prism in the dormitory one dark
night. Or better still, place a prism near to the
keyhole in the door connecting their room to the
dormitory and shine a light through the keyhole.

Maybe they could do an experiment on the quiet and if it worked, hopefully it would scare the pants off the girls in the dorm. "Please Miss Crilly, does the prism have to be as big as that one to produce the same effect?" she asked.

"No, size doesn't matter," replied the teacher, pleased with Judith showing an interest.

About the same time as Miss Crilly was revealing the secrets of white light to her class, Eilís and Kelly, who had been on an errand in Drogheda for Sr Gobnait, came staggering out of one of the shopping centres laden down with two huge parcels.

"These cushions are very heavy, Eilís, I hope we make it to the bus," panted Kelly.

"Of course we will," replied Eilís bracingly. "We couldn't pass up the chance of getting such a bargain. They're perfect for our Wiccan meetings. I'm really looking forward to using them, aren't you?"

"Definitely," replied Kelly. "One thing worries me Eilís. I was afraid to ask Clem about it, she knows so much about everything, I feel quite dumb at times."

"I know how you feel," sighed Eilis. "What's your worry though?"

Kelly looked embarrassed, then she blurted out "I know what a witch is, but not a Wiccan. What's the difference?"

Eilís laughed. "Is that all? Wiccans are good, in tune with Nature, only ever work good magic. They'd never harm anyone. They worry about their *Karma*."

"What's *Karma*?" asked Kelly. "Have we all got one?"

Eilís looked wise. "I'm not sure. Clem has one, she talks a lot about it. Do you understand about Wiccans now, Kelly?"

"I think so. It sounds fun anyway!"

"It does, doesn't it. Poor Clem, wasn't it terrible the way she was treated at her last school, just because she wanted to make a special study of Nature and herbs. Schools are so prejudiced, aren't they? Always the same old subjects," said Eilís in an aggrieved tone of voice.

"Usual thing of course, putting women down. They'll be a subject at colleges one day. Herbs I mean, not women," replied Kelly seriously.

"Absolutely. We'd better keep it to ourselves all the same. I don't want trouble, Sr Gobnait is a very reactionary type. I'd hate to lose the lead dancer in the pageant as well," replied Eilís thoughtfully. "I adore the part."

"You're brilliant at it too," said Kelly loyally. "Look, there's a beauty shop. I must get some eye make-up and maybe a lipstick. Let's go in."

"Good idea. I'm sure I need moisturiser. I hope Clem hurries up with her beauty spells, we all could do with it," said Eilís. "Whatever happens, don't let me forget Gobnait's parcel. That's why we're in Drogheda, remember!"

Kelly laughed as they went into the shop. "Poor old Gobnait! Little does she know what plans we have for this term," she said. "She'd have a fit if she knew that we've formed the Wiccans of St Brigid's!"

7

Nuala and the Seven Wigs

On the following day when Nuala arrived at the concert hall for the first rehearsal of the pageant, Mrs Horan, the English teacher who had written the script, was standing up on the stage deep in conversation with the producer, Mrs Cuddy, who taught drama, and her assistant Miss McCarthy.

The girls in the body of the hall were standing around in groups talking quietly. Nuala, spying Monica and Gwendoline, went over and joined them.

"Hi Nuala," said Gwendoline. "In case you don't realise it, we are part of the group who were picked to represent some of the early pupils in the school."

"I don't think we are the very first group," explained Monica "But certainly judging by the uniforms it was a very long time ago!"

"We were picked because of our long hair, which we wear plaited," said Gwendoline. "You should see the uniforms we'll be wearing, Nuala, you'd scream! They are dull brown, down to our ankles and quite shapeless."

"They sound ghastly," agreed Nuala. "Is that the whole uniform, you don't wear anything else?"

Gwendoline frowned. "No, I don't think so. That's all we've tried on anyway."

A door at the side of the stage opened and a lithe figure dressed in a black leotard and tights, and a multicolored scarf swathed around her slender waist, bounced in.

"I'm late, forgive me my dears," she said in a deep voice to the waiting teachers. "Dublin traffic gets more abominable every day."

"Who is that?" asked Monica, wide eyed.

"She, I think, is Miss Catt, the dance director," replied Nuala in a low tone. "And isn't she well named?"

Monica grinned. "She looks just like one, now that you mention it, doesn't she, Gwendoline?" she said, nudging her friend who agreed enthusiastically.

Mrs Cuddy stepped forward and clapped her hands. Everyone stopped talking and turned towards the stage.

"Would the dance team please come up here and meet Miss Catt," she called.

Immediately, six girls, led by Eilís Dunne, detached themselves from the crowd and walked up the steps to the stage. Nuala, idly looking at

58

them as they passed by her, suddenly stiffened. Surely, she thought, there was something familiar about the runners that two of the team were wearing. She craned her neck, noting with satisfaction that Eilís Dunne and Tara Whelan, both sixth years, were wearing runners with light strips on them. Narrowing her eyes, she scrutinised their legs, but couldn't decide in the short time available to her whether either of them belonged to the intruder in the bedroom.

Five minutes later Mrs Cuddy called Nuala up and handed her over to Miss McCarthy briskly ordering, "Sarah, take Nuala off to see if there's anything suitable in the wardrobe room for her costume. There's simply masses of stuff in there." Seeing the startled look on Nuala's face she laughed and said, "I think a wig will be essential, a good long one. Red, if possible."

"Yes Diana," said the assistant. "What about the costume itself?"

"Oh, flowing draperies, panels of chiffon, pastel colours giving a fluid line," replied Mrs Cuddy masterfully, before turning to her next task in hand.

Nuala, hurriedly following Miss McCarthy backstage and over to the room where all the costumes were stored, remembered how she had helped Sr Patrick the previous term to tidy up this room.

"Excuse me, Miss McCarthy," she said. "I know where the wigs are kept."

"Do you Nuala? Great. You root out a few and I'll look around for the costumes. Somehow I don't think we'll find anything here," she said, sighing deeply.

Nuala rushed over to where the wigs were kept. If she didn't take her chance now she felt she'd never get another. When she had selected seven wigs, she put a red one on her head, and taking another red wig with her, she went to where Miss McCarthy was dutifully, if unenthusiastically rummaging through rows of costumes.

"I've found some wigs, is it all right if I take them somewhere and try them on? I would like to get the best one for the part," Nuala said in an innocent voice.

The teacher looked over at her. "That wig is very good, I'm sure it will do," she said. "Turn around. It's certainly long enough."

Nuala swiftly switched wigs, saying "What about this one? Could I go and look at myself?"

"The first one is the better of the two, but certainly go and look at yourself. Don't be long, Mrs Cuddy might be here soon," Miss McCarthy warned in a kind voice.

"I'll be back in a minute," promised Nuala, speeding back to where she had left the wigs. Hastily she stuffed them into a plastic bag she had brought for the purpose. Then she ran all the way to Annie's Pocket, praying that she wouldn't bump into any of the teachers who might query her actions.

Throwing the bag of wigs into her wardrobe, she put on the first wig again and took a hasty glance at herself in the mirror. Thinking that she looked like a witch, she hurried quickly back to where she had left Miss McCarthy.

Nuala was just in time. She had hardly reached the teacher's side when the door opened and in came Mrs Cuddy, all brisk and business like.

"That wig is very good," she said to Nuala. "Hold on to it. Any luck with costumes, Sarah?"

"Not really Diana," said Miss McCarthy in a subdued voice. "There's masses of them all right, but nothing that I would think suitable."

"That's it then. I'll tell Sr Gobnait we'll have to order a few. You may go now, Nuala, I think Miss Catt may want to speak to you," and with that, she bustled out of the room again.

Nuala went back to the hall where Miss Catt could be seen tripping lightly all over the stage, watched intently by the dancing team who were now wearing proper dancing shoes. Nuala glanced at the row of runners sitting to one side of the hall, checking that two of them had their incriminating light strips on them.

The bell rang for break then. Nuala, feeling

satisfied with her morning's work, went off to meet Aileen and Judith to tell them the good news.

They sat out in the sun and watched the Boyne flow smoothly by while Nuala told of her experiences at the rehearsal. Josie, who had gone off to the tuck shop, was late in joining them.

"Nuala," she cried on arrival, "do you remember telling us to look out for fifth or sixth years with runners that had light strips on the heel? Well, I was in the tuck shop and Sharon Kennedy and that friend of hers Lisa Shevlin came in, and they were both wearing runners like that!"

"Four of them, the plot thickens," said Nuala dramatically.

"What's she on about?" asked Josie, looking puzzled. Nuala had to recount her morning's adventures once again.

"Brilliant!" said Josie. "Though how I'm going to fit a wig on over my mop, I don't know. Anyway, did you notice any costumes that would be useful to us?"

"I hadn't a chance to look for them," confessed Nuala. "They have to order my own costume because there's nothing suitable in stock."

"I don't suppose you could order seven more like it?" suggested Judith. "They sound just like *Banshee* outfits to me."

Nuala laughed and shook her head. "No chance of that. Mrs Cuddy is definitely not the sort to play games with."

"Pity," said Josie. "What exactly does your part consist of, Nuala? What exactly do you do?"

"Well," replied Nuala. "The whole pageant is composed of a series of acts depicting scenes about the history of the school. Someone had the bright idea of linking these acts with songs about the history of the area around here. There are four of us singers. I think we are meant to be the personification of the spirit of St Brigid's."

"It sounds pretty ghastly to me," said Josie, always candid. "But no doubt parents and others will think it beautiful."

"I hear that Sr Gobnait is crazy about it," said Judith, "and she's invited all sorts of big shots to the first night."

"So they say," agreed Nuala. "I just shudder to think what I'll look like flitting around the stage in a long red wig and pastel draperies, singing about St Patrick's visit to *Tara*."

They were all startled by Aileen, who suddenly burst out laughing. She laughed and laughed until she got hiccups. As Nuala, grinning in sympathy, thumped her back, Judith asked impatiently,

"What's the joke? Share it with us, please."

Before Aileen could reply, Gwendoline's anguished voice broke in from behind them, "Oh Aileen, how can you laugh at such a time? I've just heard that they're putting on that super *Why Cases* episode tomorrow night and there's no way we can get to see it!"

Just then the bell rang and break was over.

"I really can't explain," said Aileen to Judith as they hurried along the corridor to their next class. "It was just the thought of Nuala in that getup driving the men in the audience mad with her beauty."

Judith grinned "I can just imagine it. Perhaps we should warn Sr Gobnait," she said. "She could always blindfold them!"

8

Wiccans and Why Cases

That night in the dormitory, Gwendoline drifted off to sleep blissfully unaware that her remarks about the *Why Cases* had sparked off a fierce determination in the *Banshees* to hold their first meeting, primarily for the purpose of daring two of their members to sneak down to the Religion room on the following night and video the programme in question.

As Nuala had explained to the club members at an emergency meeting held earlier that evening, as they consumed their supper of orange squash and plain biscuits,

"We have the wigs, we have the key of the door to the tower, and now, thanks to the brilliance of the twins, we have these super masks," she said in a low tense voice. "All we need now is robes. Any ideas? No Aileen, not plastic sacks."

Eithne and Fidelma, having successfully badgered their long-suffering mother into providing the masks, smiled complacently, feeling deserving of Nuala's praise. Under the impression that she was getting the masks for the pageant, she had managed to acquire eight elegant silver and black masks which would have graced a masked ball at Versailles itself.

Aileen, munching her biscuit mutinously, made no reply to this tactless remark, while Josie whispered to Judith,

"Dressing gowns, just for tonight. What do you think?"

Judith agreed and they both urged Nuala and the others to accept this suggestion for the first meeting.

They didn't need much urging. Everyone was just dying to see the much publicised episode of the *Why Cases*, so it was arranged.

"Exactly one hour after lights out, we meet," Nuala whispered to the Murrays, who nodded happily in reply. "Don't fall asleep," she warned them.

It was definitely going to be an eventful night for the east tower of St Brigid's. As the *Banshees* impatiently counted the minutes until they could get up and robe for their inaugural meeting, the sixth year Wiccan sisterhood were slowly creeping up the narrow stone staircase in the tower. They were led by Clementine of the flowing black hair, wearing her signs of the Zodiac cloak and proudly carrying aloft a deep metal saucer of oil in which burned a bright flame. She had forbidden the use of torches, saying that only the *Sacred Flame* could be used to illuminate their way.

Eilís and June, burdened with four heavily embroidered and tasseled purple velvet cushions, panted a little behind their leader. Kelly, stumbling in the rear and laden with plastic bags, secretly wished that she had brought her torch with her. The *Sacred Flame* not only didn't throw enough light for her to see by, it also cast weird shadows on the walls of the tower as they passed. There was general relief when Clem opened the door of the top room and led the way in.

The room was about the same size as their own bedroom, which they had expected, but with a major difference. The air was stale up there and a pall of thick dust covered everything.

Clem, holding the flame up high, looked around her and commented happily, "This will be perfect for our meetings, it's obvious no one ever comes here. We'll never be disturbed."

Just behind her June gave a nervous start. "What's that?" she quavered, plucking at Clem's precious robe with one hand and pointing across the room with the other.

"What's what?" asked Clem, pushing her hand away and walking towards the wall June had pointed to. "It's probably some old furniture covered with sheets and things," she said shortly.

"Thank goodness," replied June, recovering her spirits. "I thought for a moment that it was a man crouching ready to spring on us."

Eilís laughed nervously and said "What an awful thought."

Clem said nothing. She had pulled the dust covers from the thing against the wall and was rooting around, raising quite a lot of dust as she did so.

"I was right, there are some old presses and even a wardrobe here," she exclaimed in a pleased voice, before sneezing several times.

Eilís and June, still clutching their precious cushions, went over to join her. Kelly started rooting through one of her many plastic bags for the seven candles she had brought. Just as she announced in a pleased voice that she had them, Clem produced a large wooden box and said,

"We can use this for our table."

So Kelly placed her seven candles on the box around the *Sacred Flame*, and Clem graciously lit them. The dust sheets were then spread on the floor around the table. June and Eilís dropped their cushions down on the sheets.

When they were all seated around the table, Clem reached under her cloak, producing a bag which she placed in front of them. Straining forward, the other three could see that it was covered with the signs of the Zodiac as well.

A little sigh came from Eilís, who thought this was obviously going to be really something. Under the fascinated gaze of the sisterhood, Clem carefully opened the bag, taking two objects from it. To their amazement, she then held one of the objects up in front of her and gazing into it, calmly combed her hair.

"The light here isn't the best for this kind of thing," she commented "But one should always try and look one's best for the Craft." Then she returned the comb and mirror to the bag. Sensing, perhaps, their disappointment at this action, she rooted under her cloak again, this time producing a square plastic container.

"If only we had a proper cauldron here!" she said passionately. "It's impossible to do spells properly with a plastic substitute."

"What's in the box?" asked Kelly impatiently. She was beginning to think that Clem was having them on.

"Herbs for a beauty potion. I collected them very, very early in the morning when the dew was still on them," replied Clem soulfully. "It's the next best thing to moonlight."

She opened the box and showed them a rather unappealing mass of leaves soaking in some solution.

"I'll leave it here beside the *Sacred Flame*," she said. "They have to macerate for so many hours."

As she spoke she made a kind of scattering action over the box. Instantly a dense aromatic cloud arose from it, scenting the air around them.

The three onlookers sat up. This was more like what they had come to see. Clementine, noticing their reaction, was secretly pleased. For the third time she took something from under her cloak. This time she made strange signs with it over the table.

"Wow!" cried Eilís. "It's a wand, a magic wand!"

Clem, carried away by this remark, tapped the box containing the beauty potion two or three times with the wand, while murmuring in a low voice something which sounded like *Cigyam* as she did so.

Before their startled eyes the box moved jerkily to one side and the leaves disappeared, leaving a thick white solution behind. However, the effect was rather spoiled by the top of the wand falling off into the box, splashing some of the solution onto the *Sacred Flame*, nearly quenching it and causing a dreadful smell, making the onlookers cry out in protest.

Clem recovered quickly, pretending that it was all part of the act. She made the scattering action again and although it wasn't quite as effective as the first time, it did a lot to restore peace. Out of the corner of her eye she could see a funny expression on Kelly's face, so she quickly drew her cloak tightly around her and called for silence as she wanted to commune with the spirits.

In the flickering candlelight the shadows of the dusty room seemed to press closely around them. Kelly found it particularly unnerving, combined as it was with the dusty staleness of the air. She decided to do something about it. Taking an item out of one of the plastic bags beside her, she said in a defiant voice,

"Clem isn't the only one who has contacts. Look what I have," and she held up a funny shaped board. "Look Clem, it's a Ouijee board."

Clem, looking quite furious, replied dampingly "I'm not sure I approve of Ouijee boards, they might damage my Karma."

"What's Karma ?" asked June.

"Don't you people know anything at all?" replied Clem shortly.

"I've heard of Ouijee boards," said Eilís. "I'd love to see it in action."

Kelly was annoyed with Clem. "What do you mean by that?" she asked. "Of course we know about things, that's why I borrowed the board from my cousin."

She pushed the *Sacred Flame* and four of the candles to one side and, opening the board out flat, she placed it on the table. The other girls could see that it was divided into squares. Each square had a letter of the alphabet on it.

Scrabbling in her plastic bag again, she produced a glass which looked a little like a magnifying glass with an arrow marked on it. Placing this on the board, she said,

"OK, this is what we do. Each of you place your hand on this glass and concentrate on it. I will ask a question and the arrow should then move around the board. I will write down the letter that it points too and in that way we will receive its message. Are you joining in with us, Clem?"

Although Clem had intended to proudly disassociate herself from them, when it came to the point her curiosity got the better of her, so she rather haughtily agreed to join in.

The others, concentrating hard, watched with bated breath as Kelly intoned in a deep voice, "Is there anybody there?"

At first nothing happened at all. Then, just as they were about to give up, the glass moved under their hands and to their great excitement, the arrow jerked and pointed in the direction of "S". Then it moved slowly from letter to letter.

"S", wrote Kelly excitedly in a note book she had brought with her. "S", then "I", then "L" . . . "L" . . . "Y'. "That sounds like *Silly*."

"Who are you?" stammered Kelly, her mouth feeling strangely dry.

The arrow moved again, this time it pointed to "B". Kelly wrote down the letters again, but this time she sounded puzzled. "Silly Billies," she said at last. "What could that mean?"

"It's an old fashioned term," said Clementine. "It means that we are being called silly fools, I suppose."

Kelly was mad. She looked at Clem. "If this is your idea of a joke, I don't think much of it," she stormed. "You must be interfering with it."

Clem was astonished. "Me?" she cried. "I told you it wasn't a good idea, but of course I never interfered with it!"

"I don't believe you," said Kelly tight-lipped. "This time we'll do it without her."

So the three girls put their hands on the glass again. As before, it didn't react for a while. Then suddenly it seemed to go wild. Kelly wrote down the letters, then her face fell.

"Gob ackt oyo urb eds," said Kelly perplexed. "What does that mean?"

"You have to mess around with the letters," said June. "Go – Back – To – Your – Beds," she said at last "I can't understand this, that's not a message."

Although Clem was as surprised as the others were, she just couldn't keep her mouth shut. "You shouldn't mess around with things you don't understand," she said in a superior voice. "Anyway, I'm taking its advice, I'm going back to bed. I have to think of my Karma." At that she bent down and blew the seven candles on the table out.

"What's Karma ?" asked June for the second time.

Kelly, stuffing all her things back into their plastic bags, snatched up the *Sacred Flame* and made for the door of the room, leaving them in darkness.

As she furiously made her way down the stairs, a strange noise from below arrested her flight. Peering down into the dark well of the stairs, she saw something very weird looking up at her, making her heart jump into her mouth with a loud thump. The thing seemed to glow in the dark. Then, as suddenly as it appeared, it disappeared again.

Kelly turned and fled back to the top room. Her three friends were still standing in shocked silence in the dark there. Kelly rushed over and, clutching the mystified Eilís by the arm, jabbered frenziedly at her.

"It was a faceless fiend, Eilís. A horrible faceless fiend. I saw it down at the bottom of the stairs grinning up at me, then it disappeared."

Though no one ever spoke to each other about what happened next, each of the four of them distinctly heard the sound of laughter reverberate through the room for a few seconds. Screaming, they ran back down the stairs to their own bedroom.

9

The Case of the Lunatic Laundry

In the darkness of their bedroom, the Banshees, complete with blonde wigs and silver masks, waited impatiently for Nuala to return from checking that it was safe for them to go up to the top room of the tower for their meeting.

The reason for this caution was that when they had all crept out of their cubicles sometime earlier, they had found that the keyhole in the door to the staircase was blocked up by something resembling a mixture of chewing gum and blue tack.

It had taken Josie and Aileen ages to pick it all out of the keyhole. Eventually it was clear and the key turned in the lock. As a result, Nuala had whispered that she would check first that all was clear.

Suddenly she whisked herself back into the room again, very gently closing the door behind her. "Phew! Was that a lucky escape!" she exclaimed quietly, taking off her mask and gently fanning her face with it. "It was just as well I checked and now I know why that girl was here the other day, to block up the keyhole."

"Don't be so mysterious, Nuala," complained Judith. "Just tell us what happened out there."

"Come on Nuala, spill the beans," urged Josie.

"Well," replied Nuala "When I opened the door I thought I heard funny noises coming from the top of the stairs, so I quickly stepped back into the doorway behind me and waited. The next minute what did I see but Kelly Wallace coming down the stairs carrying a kind of flaming torch, as far as I could make out. Suddenly she stopped and peered down as if she had seen a ghost or something. Without thinking I flashed my torch straight at her and with that she just turned and rushed back up the stairs. Then I slipped back in here."

"Wow!" said Aileen. "Those sixth years are using the top room for some game of their own. Good thing you saw her first."

Nuala nodded. "Just as well we didn't go up earlier. If they had caught us we would have been in big trouble."

"I suppose they bunged up the lock so that we wouldn't hear any noises as they passed up and down," said Judith. "And maybe report it to someone."

"It looks like that," replied Nuala "Or else they wanted to make sure they wouldn't be followed.

They also must not have had permission to go up there either."

"What about our own meeting?" whispered Ciara. "Will we have to cancel it?"

Nuala considered for a moment. "No, definitely not," she replied in a low voice. "This is a tower room too, we can have our meeting here, for tonight anyway."

"Good stuff, Nuala," said Aileen. "Come on you lot, sit on the floor in a circle."

"Maybe we could hold our meetings in a different place each time," suggested Judith.

"Good idea," agreed Nuala. "That way we'll be less easy to trace. Anyway, sit down now."

So they all sat down on the floor. Then Nuala produced the precious book and by the light of her torch read out softly, "What are we here for?"

"To plan a dare," They all whispered back.

"What is our aim?" she asked.

"Friendship and fun," came the whispers from the darkness around her.

"What is our name?"

"*Banshees* of St Brigid's!" was the enthusiastic reply.

Judith's apple-green quilted wash bag, which had been pressed into service, was then passed around the group and each girl picked out a rolled up scroll of paper from it.

"I've got it!" announced Aileen excitedly.

"Me too!" said Ciara in a quavering voice. She wasn't very keen on doing the dares part of the club.

"Now *Banshees*," said Nuala briskly, "You know what you have to do. Take this blank video tape that I took from the science room and video the *Why Cases* at 10pm tomorrow night, on Network 8. Don't fail or else! I promise the punishment will be horrendous."

"We won't," replied Aileen cheerfully. "I'm only dying to see the case of the *Lunatic Laundry* myself."

"Thank goodness that's over!" said Josie yawning hugely. "Let's get back to bed, the heat from this wig is just killing me."

Suddenly everyone felt terribly tired so, without further delay, they all went off to their cubicles and were soon fast asleep.

About 9:30pm on the following evening, Aileen and Ciara, after a somewhat perfunctory wash and change, could be seen slipping quietly through St Anne's dormitory in their dressing gowns. As they had picked a time when everyone was preparing for bed, no one saw them pass.

Their good luck held as they swiftly sped through the castle, leaving the dormitories behind and going downstairs to where the Religion room was situated quite near the common rooms.

On reaching their destination, Aileen, unlocking the door, cautiously led the way in, flashing her torch around her as she did so. Not surprisingly, the room looked just the same as it always did. Teacher's desk and blackboard to one side of the room, with a large white press containing the television and video equipment on the other. And rows of chairs facing them both.

"The TV is plugged in," said Ciara. "Miss Connolly must have been taping something for tomorrow's class."

"Good stuff," said Aileen, taking a blank tape out of her dressing gown pocket. "It'll save us a bit of trouble. Here, you take the torch," and she handed the torch over to Ciara.

"Let me see now," murmured Aileen thoughtfully. "This VCR has a VideoPlus system. Now, I'll just pop my tape in thus. Oh no, there's one in there already!"

She removed this tape, placing it on top of the video, then she deftly slotted her own one into the machine.

"Now Ciara," she ordered cheerfully, "Shine the torch over here, not at the window! I will now turn on the TV and set the timer to record the brilliant, wonderful, one and only *Why Cases*."

Ciara did as instructed, and within seconds Aileen had set the timer to record the programme. Just then, Ciara said in a worried voice "Aileen, do you realise that its already ten o'clock? We'd better get back to the dorm as soon as possible, we might be missed."

"Is it really?" said Aileen, not noticeably fussed. "Perhaps I'd better check that the video is working before we go. I won't be long, I promise."

As she spoke, the fuzzy screen cleared and the familiar logo of Network 8 appeared emblazoned across it. A voice announced brightly,

"And now we join Wolf Damper and Evadne Tully for another episode of the *Why Cases – Tales of the Inexplicable*."

Aileen had been quite sincere when she had promised Ciara that she wouldn't be long. However, once she saw the dark saturnine features of Wolf Damper sitting at his desk, the book of *Why Cases* in front of him and heard him saying in his rich, unctious voice, "Tonight we shall find out the WHY behind the *Case of the Lunatic Laundry*," she was hooked. All thoughts of leaving the room fled from her mind. Ciara didn't make any protest either. She just switched off the torch and sat down beside Aileen, who was eagerly waiting for the story to unfold.

It started with the moon shining brightly down on a large ivy covered building bearing the name of Roswell College. Moving swiftly through this college full of sleeping students, the camera eventually came to a stop in what was obviously the laundry room, judging by the row of washing machines lined up against one of the walls there. As they watched, a ball of white light appeared hovering over the machines, moving from one to another. As soon as the light reached the last machine, the whole row sprang into life, not only going through the motion of washing clothes, but literally bucking and rearing around the room in a weird dance.

"Wow!" breathed Aileen. "Just look at those suds, they're spilling all over the place!"

It was true. The frenzied machines now were covered with foaming suds, spilling and splashing out from them and all over the floor. At this point the door of the room burst open, revealing the shocked faces of a group of girls in various types of night attire.

The machines were now seen to be back in their usual inert state against the wall; even the soapy water had disappeared completely from the floor. After a few minutes, the mystified watchers went quietly away.

This scene was repeated twice more. On the third occasion one of the girls, braver than the rest, suddenly darted into the room and pulled at the door of the first machine.

"Look!" she shouted wildly, "It's hot and full of jeans and things!"

A mass of clothes fell out at her feet. Picking up what she thought were a pair of jeans, she held them up to prove her point. To her amazement, all the watching girls instantly fled the room screaming hysterically. She examined her find more closely.

"Oh my gosh!" she said in a strangled voice. "These jeans have five legs in them instead of two, and one is shorter than the rest!" The strange garment fell limply from her hand as she fell lifeless to the floor.

Wolf Damper could be seen again, still at his desk. "The following day the college principal, Dr C Kent, called on my esteemed colleague, Dr Evadne Tully for help. They were old college buddies," he announced.

The telephone ringing interrupted him. Snatching it up he spoke smartly into it. "Damper here." He listened intently, then he spoke again. "Right, I'll meet you in Roswell College within the hour."

Ciara and Aileen sighed happily as they leaned back in their seats in the front row of chairs.

Meanwhile, outside the castle, Miss Connolly, who was returning from visiting friends, noticed a light shining in a window where it shouldn't have been. That's definitely my Religion room, she thought. I wonder who could be there? I'd better check it out anyway. She opened the side door into the castle with her key and hastened up the stairs towards the room in question.

Although Aileen and Ciara were completely absorbed in their favorite programme, some instinct for self-preservation kept Aileen on the alert. Just as Wolf Damper was poised to rush into the laundry room, a warning had come from E Tully – who was swinging from one of the ceiling lights in the passage behind him –

"Beware, Wolfie!" she had screamed "Never stand between a hippo and its water hole!"

In the breathless hush that followed as Wolf Damper slowly turned around and viewed the simply enormous blue hippopotamus which was charging towards him, Aileen became aware of footsteps walking along the corridor not too far away from them.

"Turn off the TV," she hissed to Ciara, then she raced over and quietly locked the door and removed the key from it.

Now that the TV was off, the room seemed very dark and Ciara could hear her own frightened breathing, especially as brisk footsteps could be heard coming nearer and nearer and then stopping outside their door. The handle turning and the door being rattled nearly made her scream, but by stuffing her handkerchief into her mouth, she managed to stifle any sound. Just as Aileen was beginning to think that all was lost, they heard the sound of a nearby door opening, followed by a lot of laughter and talk.

The person moved away from their door and must have asked someone a question, for then to their relief they heard a familiar voice saying,

"The *Why Cases* Miss Connolly. We've special permission. You should watch them, they're really brilliant."

"It must have been the light in your common room I saw then," said the teacher. "Good night girls, don't delay."

Five minutes later everyone had gone.

"Ciara, you have the torch," whispered Aileen. "The programme must be over as the others are gone. Switch the tapes. We'd better get going too."

Ciara hastened to obey. In her nervous state, she fumbled with the tapes, knocking them both off the video and dropping her torch on the floor. However, with Aileen's help, she found the torch and, by its light, slotted the first tape back into the video and gave the second one to Aileen to take back with her.

As they hurried back to Annie's Pocket, Ciara confided to Aileen that she felt very sick.

"I'm not surprised," said Aileen. "Anyway, if we're caught, we can truthfully say that I was taking you to get help."

Ciara smiled wryly. "It wouldn't be a lie, I do feel awful."

"I don't feel that good myself," replied Aileen "Especially when I consider that we owe our miraculous escape to that awful Sharon Kennedy, of all people."

An Inexplicable Episode

Aileen woke up on the following morning to the sound of Judith calling her name.

"Wake up, Aileen, wake up," she urged. "Did you get the *Why Cases* taped?"

Aileen sat up, rubbing her eyes. "We did," she said yawning. "I'm so tired, what I do for my friends. I'm just exhausted."

"That's because you were back so late. What kept you?" asked Judith. "I fell asleep waiting for you."

Aileen looked thoughtfully at her, bearing in mind that Ciara had agreed with her that they shouldn't tell anyone that they had seen most of the programme already. "Oh, we were nearly caught by Miss Connolly," she said, jumping out of bed. "Go on Judith, I'll give you the details later. I have to dress now."

Judith went off to tell to Nuala and the others the good news. It wasn't until the mid-morning break that the *Banshees* could get together and hear the details.

Aileen handed the tape over to Nuala. "Here you are, mission accomplished," she said.

"Great, how did you get it?" asked a surprised Nuala.

"I had to leave the key back this morning anyway," Aileen answered, evading the question. Then she hastily told the story of how the teacher had tried to get into the Religion room.

"Wow!" gasped Josie "Were you petrified?"

"I was," agreed Ciara. "I hope I don't pull out any more dares."

"Those lucky sixth years," said Deirdre. "I wish we could get permission to watch whatever we liked."

"The big question now is, when can we get to see it ourselves?" said Nuala "And where? We haven't a video on our common room set, as you well know."

"The geography room," suggested Eithne.

"'Fraid not," said Josie. "It's out of order."

"What about the Religion room then?" said Judith.

"No, no, I couldn't," said Ciara emphatically. "The strain would be too much. I'll never forget last night."

"All right, keep your hair on," said Nuala. "We'll all have to just think about it then. I have a pageant rehearsal after break, and I shall bend my mind and energies to the problem."

"You're so lucky, Nuala," said Aileen. "Missing class. I did my study so badly last night too."

The bell rang then, so they all went slowly back to their classrooms again. Rehearsals ran late that day, and Nuala was one of the last to sit down to dinner.

"Hi Nuala, have you heard the news?" said Aileen to her as she sat down with her plate of food.

"What news?" asked Nuala. "I've just come from a pretty intensive rehearsal."

"Well," said Aileen, passing her the salt, "Miss Crilly is absent today for some reason, and we haven't any science class this afternoon. Hurrah! Hurrah!"

"What are we having instead?" asked Nuala, amused at the expression of joy on Aileen's face.

"We have to go to the Religion room, of all places," replied Aileen. "Miss Connolly will be taking us, so it should be a fairly easy afternoon."

"No wonder you're looking so pleased," said Nuala, smiling rather absently at her.

As they were leaving the dining-room, Judith slipped her hand in Nuala's arm, enquiring in a low voice, "Are you worried about something Nuala?"

Nuala looked surprised. "Not really, why do you ask?" she said.

"You weren't your usual chatty self at dinner. I just wondered . . . " said Judith.

"It's funny you should say that," said Nuala. "I was thinking about that silver shield, you know the blank one in the museum. I must ask Miss Ryan if they have found out anything more about the missing name."

"Good idea. I'd forgotten all about it. What put it into your mind, I wonder?" said Judith.

"I don't know, but I must tell you that I saw the girl from the library again," said Nuala.

"You mean the one who gave us the book?" said Judith. "How interesting. Where did you see her?"

"I was standing in the wings during rehearsal today. We actually were using the stage, you see. Anyway, I was all alone waiting for my cue, when I heard my name called. When I turned around there was that girl standing there smiling at me. 'Have you read the book?' she asked. So I told her I was reading it but I hadn't got very far because it's a bit hard to read as it's faded in parts."

"You're not serious! What did she say to that?" asked Judith.

"Well, she agreed, saying that it was written a very long time ago, of course, and parts were bound to be faded. Then she asked me if I was enjoying it. So, of course I said we were and did she want it back soon. Shaking her head she said, 'No, keep it for as long as you like.' Then she smiled and said,

'I'm glad you enjoy friendship and fun,' adding that she had always been like that too. Just then I heard my cue, and I had to go out and sing. When I got back again, she had gone."

"What a pity, I don't suppose you found out her name either?" asked Judith.

"No, I didn't," said Nuala. "I wonder what she was doing at rehearsals all the same."

Aileen and Josie joined them then and the conversation turned to other things.

When the whole class was sitting in the Religion room that afternoon, Miss Connolly announced brightly that she had arranged a rare treat for them.

"I've taped a special teenage programme for you. *From Here to Maturity* it's called, and I know you'll enjoy it."

Outwardly the class responded like a row of graven images, inwardly they were mostly a mixture of bored indifference.

Having rewound the video and set it in motion, she announced that she would have to leave them for a while. Grainne, as class captain, was in charge. She expected them to be mature and behave well. Then she left.

They all saw the Network 8 logo appear without any great expectation of pleasure. Suddenly, as they listlessly watched the beginning of the programme, a wave of excitement rippled through the room as the startled watchers heard the *Why Cases – Tales of the Inexplicable* announced, followed by the familiar tones of Wolf Damper explaining about Roswell College and its troubles with the laundry room.

"Cool, cool," was a refrain heard from around the room. Needless to say, no one was more surprised than the *Banshee* club, especially Aileen and Ciara. Not that they were complaining, quite the reverse in fact. Everyone settled comfortably in their chairs, prepared to enjoy this brilliant, totally unexpected treat.

It was very near the end of the programme when something occurred to Nuala.

Wolf Damper, standing in a large library, was saying to someone invisible there, "This case bears the stamp of a person we've met before in the *Pulverized Publisher*, for example. Especially with all those jungle beasts roaming the building. Would you agree?"

"You could be right. The *Noxious Newsagent* springs to mind also," said Tully's voice from the top of a large bookcase.

"That's it Tully, clearly the work of Weirdo Kelvin! How shall we proceed?"

"I've got it!" cried Tully triumphantly, jumping lightly down from her perch. "At last I've found it!"

"You have, what is it?" asked Damper puzzled.

"It's my mom's special recipe for *Lemon Meringue Pie*, Wolf," she replied happily. "It's simply out of this world."

"Dr Tully, keep your mind on your work please," said Damper in a shocked voice. "Be careful with that recipe all the same, *Lemon Meringue Pie* is a favorite of mine too."

At this moment, Nuala edged the other tape out of her folder and looked at it. *From Here to Maturity* was neatly printed on its label. She pointed this out to Aileen, who only grinned and said,

"It's a miracle!"

The programme was barely over when the teacher returned, apologising for her tardiness. "Well girls," she asked, "How did you like the programme? Do you think that it will help your problems?"

"Brilliant, Miss Connolly, it was brilliant," came enthusiastically from all over the room.

The teacher was pleased.

"When can we see the second half?" asked Gwendoline with shining eyes.

"Second half? I didn't know that there was one," replied the surprised teacher.

"There is definitely, it said so at the end," said Gwendoline.

"In that case, I shall certainly look up the TV guide and tape it," replied Miss Connolly.

The bell rang and they all got up to go. In the general exodus from the room, Nuala managed to unobtrusively change the tape, wondering as she did so would the teacher be suspicious when she found out the tape didn't need rewinding. Anyway, no one would ever know who had switched the tapes, as the *Banshees* were all sworn to secrecy.

Many and varied were the comments the girls made as soon as they were out of earshot. No one really thought that Miss Connolly had meant to show the *Why Cases* to them.

Gwendoline rushed up to where Nuala, Aileen and Judith were discussing whether getting the second part taped would be the subject of a new dare or whether Aileen and Ciara should be asked to repeat their performance of the night before.

"We'll just have to tape the second part," Aileen was saying "But I think some one else will have to do the job. It's only fair."

"Aileen, Aileen." called Gwendoline "Wasn't that brilliant! I'm only dying to see the second half. How do you think Miss Connolly's tape was switched and who could have done it?"

Aileen looked at Gwendoline with a very grave face. "It's only inexplicable," she pronounced solemnly. "Do you think we should call in the *Why* team to solve it for us?"

Gwendoline looked puzzled, then her face cleared. "I think that's a brilliant idea. I'd just love to speak to Wolf Damper in person," she replied enthusiastically.

11

"The Best is Yet to Come"

A few days after Aileen and Ciara's spectacular and successful completion of their dare for the *Banshee* club, Kelly Wallace went into her bedroom in the east tower full of excitement.

"Clem!" she cried "What do you think – I've just overheard Sr Gobnait tell Miss Grimes that our visit to Dublin on Friday is all fixed up . The coach is due to leave here at 2 pm, so that we can do some shopping and have a meal before the play starts."

Kelly was referring to the proposed sixth year outing to Dublin to see the play *Macbeth*, which was on the Leaving Cert course that year.

Clem looked up from the letter she was reading, her face unusually animated. "What a coincidence," she replied. "This letter is from Gareth, and he's going to the play on Friday too."

"Who is Gareth?" asked Kelly.

Clem laughed lightly. "Oh, only a boy I know. He's at Newgrange College."

Kelly was instantly all interest. "What's he like, are you an item, how long do you know him?" she rattled off quickly.

"Oh, he's just a friend," Clem replied in her usual calm way. "You may see him on Friday."

"Is he a Wiccan too?" asked Kelly eagerly.

"No, of course . . . " Clem started to reply, then quickly changed her mind to, "Well, actually he is one. And that reminds me, I might have to get some info from him. Would you help to cover up for me, if I can get to meet him?"

"Of course," replied Kelly cheerfully. "That will be no problem at all. I don't suppose we could put a spell on old Grimes, the English teacher, when we're about it, could we?"

"Wiccans don't cast bad spells on people," said Clem somewhat primly. "We only want to do good, and be in tune with nature."

"Well, it wouldn't have to be a bad spell," protested Kelly. "Just something to get rid of her for the evening. It will be brilliant to get away from school on Friday, won't it?"

"Definitely. I had a letter from my mum today as well. She worries a lot about me getting out of school."

"Lucky you," sighed Kelly enviously. "Mine only worries about me working hard for the Leaving Cert, behaving well, and not getting friendly with anyone who might lead me astray. Though how you could meet anyone like that here, I don't know."

Clem, staring into space, a peculiarly saintly expression on her face, made no reply. She was busy thinking of how alike Kelly's mother and hers were, going by her mum's letter, which she had just thrown on her bed. She must contact Gareth too, as soon as possible.

At the same time as this conversation was taking place, Nuala and Judith were talking to Miss Ryan, the history teacher, in the museum, just below the senior girls' bedroom.

"Did you ever discover the name of the *Merry Gold Medal* winner of 1896 and why her name wasn't engraved on the shield for that year?" asked Nuala.

"It's a complete mystery," said the teacher wryly. "We have found every record about the school's past, except for the prizewinners' list for 1896."

"You've narrowed it down to a list, have you then?" asked Judith.

"We have," said Miss Ryan. "You know girls, I'll be giving out the history projects in class tomorrow. I think you two should take the history of the *Merry Gold Medal* for yours. If you two put your minds to it, you probably would trace that list."

Nuala looked at Judith. "What a brilliant idea!"

she said. "I'd really like to find out who the girl was and why they didn't put her name on the shield. Wouldn't you Judith?"

"Absolutely. Thanks, Miss Ryan. We'd love to do that," said Judith.

"I do hope you find out her name. It would be the last piece in a kind of historical jigsaw," remarked the teacher. "We'd all be grateful."

The two friends left the museum shortly afterwards, all enthusiasm for the project.

"We could see ourselves as an investigative team," suggested Nuala. "And when we find it, we could write it up like that."

"Good idea," said Judith "I'm glad you said *when* we find it, not *if*. Where should we start?"

"First, I suppose we'll have to find out when the prize was started, and who thought up the whole idea," said Nuala.

When they reached the common room, Aileen met them with the good news that Gwendoline's mother had promised not only to video the second part of the *Why Cases*, but to get it to St Brigid's by the following day.

"Brilliant," said Judith. "I'm only dying to see what this Weirdo Kelvin looks like."

"Same here," said Aileen. "But the sticky question remains, where will we be able to view it?"

"You're right," said Josie from her perch on a window seat. "We can't hope for a second miracle."

"Did you hear that Miss Connolly asked Monica what she thought were the highlights of *From Here to Maturity*." chuckled Nuala. "Poor Monica nearly had a fit!"

"What did she say?" asked Judith.

"Luckily she remembered some gobbledygook about the joy of experiencing the pain of growth, or something weird like that, but she told me that it was a ghoulish moment," said Nuala.

"Wasn't Monica clever," said Aileen. "I'm afraid I would have to blurt out that the best moment for me was when Dr Tully swung from one ceiling light to another, then leant down and snatched Wolf Damper up out of the way of the charging hippos, by his hair."

"That was really brilliant," agreed Josie. "Though his head must have been really sore. I think I liked the way one minute the washing machines were jigging madly, with all the foaming water splashing all over the place, and then as soon as the door was opened, everything was perfectly quiet and back to normal again."

"Or even the part when the two blue hippos crashed into each other and exploded, turning into hundreds of lighted candles, which floated around the passage before taking the shape of a Christmas tree, then fading away," said Aileen.

"If only we had something like a *Why Case* going on in the school," sighed Josie. "It would break up the awful dullness of it all."

"No such luck," sighed Judith. "St Brigid's is such a sensible place, nothing paranormal ever happens here."

The common room door opened and Eithne, obviously full of news, stood there. "Girls," she said dramatically. "The sixth years are going to Dublin on Friday to see *Macbeth*. They don't expect to be back before midnight. What does that suggest to your innocent minds?"

"The *Why Cases*," said Nuala at once. "We can watch Gwendoline's tape on the video there!"

"Good stuff," cheered Aileen. "But we'll have to be very careful."

"Yes," agreed Nuala. "We'll have to make a plan and keep to it. First of all, Eithne, close that door behind you. We don't want anyone to overhear us."

"Thank goodness for Gwendoline's mum," whispered Ciara to Judith. "She has lifted a weight off my mind."

On the Friday evening in question, while the rest of her year were watching the curtain rise for the first act of *Macbeth*, Clem Vallely, successfully eluding the vigilant Miss Grimes, left the Gaiety theatre. Soon she was walking down Grafton Street towards Pizza King, where a tall fair boy was waiting impatiently for her.

After an enthusiastic greeting, Clem led the way into the restaurant, carefully picking a table at the back, out of sight of the door. "Have you got it, Gareth?" she asked eagerly, as soon as the waitress had taken their order.

"Got what?" he teased. "What's the girl on about?"

"Oh, Gareth, don't act the fool, you know full well what I'm on about. The book."

"Oh, the book, the one you asked me to buy for you. Let me see . . . it's here somewhere . . . " he replied, taking a slim packet out of his pocket. "I'd quite a job finding *The Complete Guide to Getting an A1 in Irish in the Leaving.*"

"Watch it!" she warned. "Any more, and I'll plaster you with the pizza, right across your face."

"Help, you've convinced me," he laughed, handing the book over to her.

Clem ripped the plastic bag open. "Brilliant!" she screeched "You got it! *Successful Spells for Every Occasion.*"

Gareth grinned at her. "What do you want that rubbish for?" he asked. "I was terrified someone would catch me buying it."

"You've no idea what a dull hole St Brigid's is," she answered, flipping over the pages of the book as she did so. "To help relieve the tediousness of it, I've formed a Wiccan society and I need the book for it."

"A what society?" he queried.

"Wiccans are kind of white witches," she

99

replied. "They do spells and worry about their Karma."

"What's a Karma?" he asked somewhat thickly, as their pizzas had arrived and he was working his way swiftly through his.

"That's the name we Wiccans use for our fate in the next state of our existence," she replied loftily, then looking at Gareth she added teasingly, "Going by the way you are stuffing that pizza in, your next reincarnation will be that of a pig, monster size."

"Is that so?" he replied indignantly. "For that I won't give you back the ring."

"You found my moonstone ring!" she cried happily. "Brilliant. It's just perfect for doing spells."

"You aren't serious about this witch thing, are you?" he asked as he passed over the ring.

Clem put it on, and waved her hand at him. "Oh, I don't know, there's a lot to be said for witches, especially Wiccans. How would you like me to put a spell on you that would make you attractive to the chicks?"

"What cheek! I'm that already. I don't need your spells," he protested.

"Don't be such a big head," she said. "I suppose I'd better go soon, I don't want old Grimes catching me out."

"Hi guys," said a strange voice "How goes it?"

Gareth looked up; he didn't seem pleased. "Hi Brian," he said. "We were just going." And before she could protest, Clem found herself out in the street again.

"What's the matter?" she asked "Who was that."

"That was snoopy Murray." he said. "He has a cousin, I believe, in St Brigid's. I don't want him blabbing to her about us."

While this conversation was taking place, back at St Brigid's Nuala and Aileen were slipping into the sixth year common room carrying a large bundle, closely followed by Judith and Eleanor Farrelly, the tallest girl in their year.

Judith placed a chair on the common room table, then the others carried both table and chair carefully and very quietly over to the window. Then Eleanor, kicking off her shoes, climbed on this edifice. Judith, standing on the table beside the chair, received the bundle from Aileen and Nuala, which when unrolled turned out to be two thick blankets pinned together. Eleanor, with Judith's help soon had this hung across the tall narrow window.

They had hardly finished putting the blackout in position when the rest of the class slipped quietly into the room in twos and threes, taking up their position on the floor in front of the television. When everyone was in place, Nuala put another rolled-up blanket against the locked door while Gwendoline slipped her tape into the video recorder and turned the machine on.

Nuala looked around the darkened room with satisfaction. "Our blackout seems effective," she said to Judith. "Let's hope all goes well."

Judith didn't pay any heed to this, she was too interested in looking at the laundry room, once again the scene of hideous, soapy suds swamping the floor as each washing machine danced, rocked and rolled around in a frenzy.

A gasp went up from the watchers as the suds suddenly came together, taking shape, twisting and turning faster and faster. The shape turned round, revealing a grinning evil face. It rose up from the floor with a loud sucking noise, then, slipping under the door of the laundry room, vanished out of sight. The washing machines slowed down, then stopped. The moonlight shone in on the now peaceful room, with its sparkling clean floor.

Back in Dublin the crowd streamed out of the Gaiety, laughing and talking. Kelly and Eilís walked among the other sixth years with worried looks. Suddenly a rather breathless Clem appeared beside them.

"How did it go?" asked the relieved Kelly quietly to her.

"Perfectly," said Clem. "How was the play?"

"Very good. I enjoyed it," said Eilís.

"You'll have to fill me in about it tomorrow." said Clem.

Neither of them liked to ask her when she would fill them in about her escapade.

Just about the time the coach was setting off on its return journey to the school, the episode of the *Why Cases* was winding to its end.

Damper and Tully, after a tortuous time, had finally trapped the elusive Weirdo Kelvin. Just as he had oozed soapily across the floor towards Tully, who was pretending not to notice him, Wolf Damper, holding an empty detergent bottle, crept up behind him and shouted their motto "The best is yet to come!"

This startled the villain, who turned and ran straight into the empty container, which Wolf promptly capped and sealed securely.

Then Wolf held up the bottle, which had "Pixie Liquid" stamped on it, and said to Dr C Kent, the college principal, "This should keep Weirdo out of mischief, but there is one thing you must know. Clothes must never be washed in that room again."

Dr Tully added her mite, "The best is yet to come," she cried.

The spell was broken by a voice announcing that Wolf Damper and Evadne Tully would return in two weeks time, when they would find out why the Rodent Ratted.

"Come on everyone," whispered Nuala. "Let's get this room back to normal, as quietly as possible."

"Yes, be careful," warned Aileen. "We don't want Sr Gobnait catching us and putting us away in Pixie Liquid bottles for the rest of the term."

12

Eithne Throws Down a Challenge

"Now Judith, let's recap what we've found out so far about the *Merry Gold Medal*," said Nuala briskly, opening the copy in which she had made copious notes about their history project.

"First of all, what do we know about its origin?" replied Judith in the same business-like voice.

"In 1876, Anastasia Merry's parents endowed a sum of money for the purpose of awarding an annual gold medal in memory of their daughter who died in her final year at St Brigid's," said Nuala, ticking off the appropriate sentences in her copy.

"What was the prize to be awarded for?" asked Judith.

"According to an old letter in the museum, Mr and Mrs Merry specified that it was to be given to the girl who was voted the nicest girl in the school by the other pupils."

"Bearing in mind that there were only forty girls at that time in the school," Judith reminded her.

"Right, it doesn't sound so far-fetched as it would now, with over three hundred of us," said Nuala. "Anyway, the following year it was awarded to one Sarah Byrne, who won easily by ten votes."

"We won't have to give all the winners' names and what they won by, will we?" asked Judith.

Nuala considered for a moment. "We'll list the prizewinners of course, but not necessarily what their score was. Anyway, remember, it won't be that long as they changed the system about thirty years ago, and now it's only given for outstanding achievement in sixth year."

"No more nice girls . . . " quizzed Judith. "Was that the reason? Would the Merrys have approved, would you say?"

Nuala grinned. "I don't suppose they were around to care. Remember, the nuns held a special meeting to decide about the change. I gathered from something Miss Ryan said, that the increase in the price of gold had something to do with it."

"Anyway, to get back to work. The prize has been awarded since 1877. We don't know about 1896, of course."

"That's what we want to find out," said Nuala. "I'd give a lot to know what happened to that prize list. At least then we'd know the girl's name, even if she had done something terrible to forfeit it."

"Maybe it just wasn't awarded," suggested Judith. "But then it would have said that on the shield, I suppose."

Nuala looked around the common room which was empty, as most people were out enjoying the lovely sunny day.

"I suggest we look into every ancient press in the castle," she said. "It's so old, there are bound to be places that dozens of lists could be lost in."

"What about looking in the old library first," said Judith. "It looked very untidy, with all those books lying around in it."

"Good idea, Judith," said Nuala. "I wonder should we ask Mrs Long or just take a chance and try and get in ourselves?"

The door of the common room opened and Eithne Murray came in. "Hi you two," she said cheerfully. "Still working on that old medal thing? Not like us. We thought that it was too nice a day to be stuck indoors, looking up details of famous past pupils."

"Have you discovered anyone famous who was at school here?" asked Nuala lazily, leaning back in her chair, not sorry to be disturbed.

"Oh yes, quite a few," replied Eithne sitting down on the couch. "But it's not half as much fun as finding things out about the present pupils of St B's. Did you know, for instance, that Kelly Wallace, Eilís Dunne, June something-or-other, and that new girl Clementine, are a crowd of witches who hold covens up in that tower room above you lot?"

Nuala was so surprised at this that she jerked up suddenly and fell off her chair, crashing to the floor.

"What!" Judith cried. "A coven of witches above our room!"

Eithne was pleased at their reaction. "Yes," she said. "And the latest is that they are now casting spells on people who annoy them."

Nuala got up slowly from the floor, feeling herself all over. "It sounds crazy to me, but then I did see Kelly Wallace on the stairs that night," she said. "How do you find out these things Eithne?"

Eithne smiled mysteriously. "I have my sources," she said.

The other two were half inclined to believe her story. Eithne was famous in the school for hearing all the gossip before anyone else.

At this Aileen and Josie joined them. "From the stunned looks on your faces, I guess Eithne has been telling you about the witches of St Brigid's," she said.

"She has," admitted Judith. "But is it true?"

"I don't know. It would fit in with the bunging up of the keyhole in our bedroom, of course," replied Aileen.

"What do witches do at coven meetings?" asked Nuala "Do they chant or cast spells or what? It doesn't seem possible to me that anyone would do that sort of thing here. Someone's having you on, Eithne."

Eithne looked around the room. "We're all *Banshees* here," she said. "I know its true about the witches. To prove it, I'll let you know when they're holding their next meeting, then I'll dare two of you to hide in that top room and listen to them. What do you think of that?"

"Fair enough," said Nuala. "You let us know and we'll hold a meeting and choose two *Banshees* to prove you're right, or even wrong."

"Good stuff," said Aileen. "It's about time for another dare, I've done my duty already, and I'd love to know what witches do in their spare time."

"Well, I hope it won't be too soon," said Nuala. "I have missed enough class with all these rehearsals. Miss Crilly was very sarcastic about my science study this morning."

"We don't hold *Banshee* meetings at class time," said Aileen. "Not that I have any objections to the idea. Imagine Sr Gobnait's face if she found us all dressed and masked heading off for one."

"Don't be a fathead," laughed Nuala. "You know I meant I don't want to lose any more sleep, as it makes me stupid at class in the mornings."

"There's the bell. Food at last!" said Eithne, rising up from the couch and leading the way out of the room.

Later on that evening, Gwendoline came up to Nuala as they were going in to study. "Nuala," she said, "Mrs Cuddy is holding a special emergency meeting at break tomorrow and she wants the whole cast of the pageant to attend it."

"Whatever for?" asked Nuala "I thought the big run through of the pageant was to be on next Friday."

"I'm not sure, but Monica says that it isn't a rehearsal, but a meeting where Mrs Cuddy will go over everyone's performance," was Gwendoline's parting reply.

"How awful," said Aileen. "Does this happen often, Nuala?"

"I'm sure its only a kind of pep talk," said Nuala. "To get us all to feel like one group, instead of individuals. It's so boring, hockey captains do it all the time."

However, when Nuala arrived in the hall next morning, she discovered that it was much worse than she had expected. Mrs Cuddy tore everyone's performance to strips, including the singers. As Nuala and the others were still reeling from this, the producer then picked out Eilís Dunne for particular attention. Not only was she dancing badly, but indeed her whole attitude was wrong, giving the impression that she was half asleep most of the time. Finally, she dismissed them with the warning that if they didn't improve, the whole production would be cancelled.

As the stunned cast silently left the hall and returned to their classrooms, Miss McCarthy, the assistant producer, said earnestly to Mrs Cuddy:

"Really Diana, I think you were much too severe on them. They're not that bad at all."

Mrs Cuddy laughed merrily. "Don't be foolish Sarah," she said. "Of course they're not bad. In fact, I'm very pleased with their work, but I've always found a good telling off at this stage works wonders! Believe me, you'll find I'm right."

Miss McCarthy, who didn't like to go against her boss, smiled faintly and said "I'm sure you're right, Diana."

All this took place at eleven in the morning. By six that evening Eithne had slipped a note into Nuala's hand saying dramatically:

"The black spot!"

"You're not serious – tomorrow night!" protested Nuala, feeling that it wasn't her day.

That evening, when they all went into study, each Banshee found a piece of paper in her desk. Written on it was

Banshee meeting tonight. Usual place, usual time.

Wigs will be worn.

By eleven that night, nearly everyone in the castle was in bed and asleep, that is, except for the occupants of Annie's Pocket. The school clock had hardly struck the hour when eight wigged and masked figures, linking hands in a circle, sat down in the centre of the room.

110

When their leader, Nuala, had finished reading out their ritual, which all answered with enthusiasm, Aileen passed around Judith's pretty wash bag with its complement of rolled up pieces of paper. There was silence for a minute, then Josie and Judith spoke together

"I've got it!" they both said.

"Well, you know what to do," said Nuala. "Tomorrow night at midnight, four witches are supposed to be holding a coven in the top room of this tower. Your job, if you agree to accept it, is to go up early, conceal yourselves somewhere in that room and find out what they are up to."

"How long should we hang around in case Eithne has got it wrong?" asked Judith, who was inclined to agree with Nuala that someone was making up the whole story.

"Twenty minutes anyway," said Nuala. "Thank goodness the weather has been so good since we came back this term. You won't be cold anyway."

"What do you mean, I've got it wrong?" said Eithne indignantly. "Don't worry Judith, they will be there."

"How can you be so sure?" asked Josie.

"I'll give you one clue. A book of spells was passed over to Clementine at the sixth year outing to Dublin, two weeks ago, by a person who had bought the book at her request. A relative of mine gave me the whole story. That's all I'll tell you." said Eithne firmly.

"Very well, we'll go," said Josie in a heroic voice. "And if we're not back by 2 am, Aileen, you can have that black velvet scarf of mine that you've always coveted. Eithne, if your story is true, we'll probably be white mice by then and I won't need it anymore."

"If you're not back by one-thirty, we'll go in search of you," said Nuala, "Armed to the teeth with hockey sticks!"

On this heartening promise, the *Banshees* retired to bed in good spirits.

13

Spies and Spells

Judith stood in the doorway of the top room in the east tower and shone her torch around its dusty environs. "Wow! Oh wow!" she cried in amazement. "Josie, just look at those brilliant velvet cushions around that wooden box there."

Josie pushed in beside her, her eyes widening at the sight of not only the cushions in question, but also the seven candles stuck in a star-shaped formation on top of the box. "There must be something in Eithne's story after all," she whispered. "We'd better look for somewhere to hide, and quickly."

Judith nodded as she swiftly closed the door behind them. When she had shone her torch around the room, she had noticed some presses grouped against one of the walls there. Now they went over and examined these presses, finding that there were four of them plus one wardrobe, all with doors that hung open. These were the presses that the Wiccans had removed the cover sheets from on the night of their first meeting there. Fortunately, they had left one large torn piece in a heap on the floor nearby.

"Now Josie," urged Judith, picking up this piece of material. "Get into that wardrobe. It seems to have lost its shelves, if it ever had any. Then I'll drape this sheet over it in such a way that they won't even notice us."

"It's very dark in here," said Josie, getting into the wardrobe. "And its very, very dirty. Aaahhh, what's that?"

Judith arranged the torn sheet carefully so that a triangular tear in it would be placed just where they could use it as a peephole and even more importantly, an airhole.

"Thank goodness we're wearing wigs and masks," said Josie, crouching uncomfortably in her hiding place and holding the door closed over with one hand. "They might protect us from the dust, and indeed, spiders. I've just disturbed one as big as a hockey ball."

"Oh, not spiders!" cried Judith, hesitating to join Josie in the wardrobe. "I simply hate them."

"Come on Judith, have sense," said Josie impatiently. "Spiders aren't half as bad as witches. You've never heard of a spider putting a spell on anyone, did you?"

Judith muttered something inaudible as she

lifted up a corner of the sheet and crawled reluctantly in beside Josie, dropping the torn sheet into place again as she did so. It was a tight fit.

"Do you think we'll ever get out of this wardrobe again?" whispered Josie good humourdly as they adjusted themselves in their confined space.

Judith didn't hear her, as she was engrossed in looking through the little peephole in the sheet. "I can't see a thing," she complained. "It's very dark out there. I hope the witches will light those candles, if they come, that is."

"Let's hope they come soon then," said Josie, groaning at the discomfort she was enduring.

She had hardly spoken when the school clock struck midnight, nearly deafening them in the process. The last reverberations had only died away when they heard the door of the room open.

Judith caught her breath in fright, completely unaware that she was squeezing Josie's arm tightly, as they heard something slowly shuffle in and across the floor of the room. Hardly daring to breathe she peeped through the jagged tear in the sheet once again. This time she could see something, a reddish glow which appeared to be bobbing around the room. It stopped and soon she could see several little tongues of flame springing up near it.

"They must have lit the candles," she breathed

in Josie's ear. Immediately Josie craned over her shoulder in an effort to see for herself.

"I think I can make out two or three faces in the light, but its all so flickery and shadowy, I just can't see who they are," she whispered in Judith's ear; this did nothing to reassure her friend at all, especially as the atmosphere was now heavy with a strong smell of incense.

After a lot more shuffling and low voiced murmurs, they were amazed to hear the lyrics of a song floating across the room to them, "She wore Black Velvet . . . "

That's not the music we agreed on," snapped someone quite loudly. "It was meant to be Celtic, mysterious, other worldly. Turn it off."

In the silence that followed, an indistinguishable murmur rose from the direction of the lights, followed by the same voice enunciating clearly.

"Remember, we've come to cast a spell that will help Eilís. She's in a bad state since that Cuddy woman criticised her dancing. We'll use the knotted cords because they intensify our powers."

The two younger girls watched wide-eyed as four robed figures moved into the centre of the room, much nearer to them. They were holding what looked like lengths of green garden cord in their upraised right hands. These cords seemed to be joined in the middle forming an elaborate web of knots. Once in formation each silent figure bent down and picked up the other end of the cord with their free hand.

Holding the web of cords quite tautly between them, they started to dance solemnly around in a circle.

"We call on the spirit of the stars which dance in the great galaxies," came a low whisper.

"We call on the spirit of the stars," echoed the other low sibilant voices.

"We call on the spirit of flowers that dance in the great meadows," whispered the first voice again.

"We call on the spirit of the flowers," echoed the others.

"We call on the spirit of the birds that dance in the great heavens," whispered one low voice again.

"We call on all the birds in the air," echoed the others loudly and enthusiastically.

As they chanted, the dance got faster and faster, making Josie and Judith feel quite dizzy as the witches whirled madly past them.

Suddenly the cords flew up in the air and the four dancers with screeches and yells fell with loud thumps and lay sprawled across the floor right in front of the mesmerised watchers crouching uncomfortably in their hideout nearby.

After a few minutes the Wiccans rose shakily from the floor, groaning and rubbing themselves all over. Their leader, who was standing near enough for Judith to recognise her, spoke quickly.

"The cords have responded. Eilís will dance with the grace of all the spirits we have called upon, from this day on."

Josie, who had been struggling to control her laughter ever since they had heard the witches thump noisily to the floor, now collapsed into wild giggles at these words. The effect on the Wiccans as Josie's merry laughter pealed out from the darkest corner of the room was dramatic.

"It's the faceless fiend," screamed Kelly, "the faceless fiend is back!"

Snatching up the lamp from the table she rushed out of the room closely followed by three panic-stricken friends.

"Josie, how could you? I don't know how they didn't catch us," reproached Judith as they stumbled stiff and sore out of their hiding place and stood looking around the room.

Josie laughed again as she remembered the antics of the so-called witches.

"I couldn't help it, Ju," she replied. "First of all they played Ring a Ring a Rosie with some cords, and then all fall down. Then if you don't mind one of them says Eilís will dance much better because of it."

"I suppose you're right," said Judith, smiling in spite of herself. "I think we should go too, they might come back again; they'll kill us if they find us here."

"Right, lead on. Just look, those great twits didn't even wait to blow out the candles," said Josie indignantly. "How careless can you get!" She bent over and blew them all out. They hurried off downstairs and within minutes were safely back in Annie's Pocket, where they were surprised to find Nuala, along with Aileen, Ciara and Deirdre waiting anxiously for them.

"Thank goodness," said Nuala. "We heard so many awful bangs and screeches coming from up there, we thought the witches must have half killed you at least!"

"That was them making the noises all right" said Judith, handing back the door key to Nuala.

"They were dancing and chanting out a spell to improve Eilís's dancing," said Josie, laughing again, as she remembered the scene upstairs. "Then something went wrong and they all crashed to the floor."

"Improve her dancing," said Nuala in surprise. "Whatever for? Eilís dances like a fairy as it is."

"The story I heard, from the usual reliable source – that is E Murray – " said Aileen "was that Mrs Cuddy tore strips of her performance the other day after rehearsal and Eilís was devastated by it."

"Mrs Cuddy tore strips off all our performances

the other day," said Nuala ruefully. "Did you get a glimpse of who the witches were?"

"I did," replied Judith. "The leader stood near enough for me to recognise her, it was Clementine. They were all dressed in long clothes."

"What's that noise?" called Deirdre sharply. "It sounded as if it came from outside there," pointing to the door leading to the stone staircase and the top room of the tower.

"Quick," whispered Nuala, "Split, everyone. We can hear the full story later on."

At once they all scurried over to their cubicles, jumping into bed and pretending to be asleep.

Meanwhile, June, who had stumbled noisily on the stairs, picked herself up and limping slightly followed Eilís into the top room of the tower, which to their surprise was in complete darkness.

"Who blew out the candles?" asked Eilís flashing her torch around the room. She had brought a torch as they weren't on Wiccan business. Clem had appeared to be asleep when she mentioned checking out the candles. Kelly was awake, but had flatly refused to accompany June and Eilís on the grounds that she was too frightened.

"We must have done it automatically as we ran out of the room," said June who was only dying to get back to bed.

"We didn't," said Eilís in a definite voice "I'm

positive of that. I wonder who did blow them out though?"

"Don't be silly, Eilís," said June, yawning. "The room looks exactly as we left it, even the cords are lying on the floor over there."

"I keep thinking of that laugh," said Eilís. "It wasn't the first time we heard it either." With that she walked over and shone her torch on the cords.

"June," she called urgently, "Come over here, look at these cords, they couldn't have fallen that way."

June went over and looked sleepily at the floor. Then she gasped. Retreating towards the door she said in a frightened voice,

"They look as if someone formed them into a giant exclamation mark! let's get out of here! I don't want to meet Kelly's faceless fiend."

"Me neither," agreed Eilís, following her friend as she high-tailed it out of the room.

Meanwhile, down in Annie's Pocket, one by one the girls pretending to be asleep were overtaken by the real thing, until only Aileen lay awake. She was reading a letter she had received from her mother only that day. *"I hope you are studying hard."* Mrs Watson had written. *"As far as I can see to get into college nowadays you need two or three A ones. At least."*

Aileen put her letter under her pillow and snuggled down into her duvet.

"Dear Mum," she said sleepily. "I haven't a chance of getting any A ones but by the time we've finished in St Brigid's, we'll be able to run a detective agency without any bother."

Soon she too, was sleeping the sleep of those who lead blameless lives.

14

The Top Room Revisited

"What a brilliant story," said Aileen, leaning back against Barney's massive trunk. "I especially liked the part where you laughed, Josie, and they all ran out of the room screaming with fright."

As soon as they had finished classes on the following day, the *Banshees* had hurried out to meet in their favourite beech tree. Then Josie and Judith had told them the full story of the adventures of the night before.

"It wasn't a bit funny at the time," said Judith solemnly. "I was terrified that they would catch us in that old wardrobe. You know we were only inches away from them there."

"I'm glad I wasn't with you," said Ciara. "I thought our dare was scary enough, I would have died with fright if I had been there last night!"

"Well, Eithne was proved right, wasn't she?" said Fidelma proudly. "She's a whizz kid at hearing the gossip isn't she?"

"She sure is," said Nuala. "What I can't understand is why they were so frightened by Josie's laugh?"

"I don't know," said Judith. "One of them screamed something about a 'faceless fiend' whatever that is, and then they all ran out."

"Who would have ever thought that our Josie would be called a 'faceless fiend'?" laughed Nuala. "Maybe your wig slipped over your face."

"They couldn't have seen me anyway, I was well hidden behind Judith," said Josie, delighted at the effect her laughter had produced on the witches.

"Hi everyone. I've got letters," called a fresh voice and Eithne's face appeared among the foliage.

Pulling herself up on the branch, she perched beside Aileen, waving some envelopes in the air. "Let me see now," she said teasingly. "What have we here . . . A letter from Judith's mum, judging by the stamp. What's this, has anyone ever heard of a Nuala O'Donnell in this school?"

Nuala and Judith lunged forward in an effort to snatch their letters from Eithne.

"Hey, go easy you two, you'll have us all in the Boyne." warned Josie.

"Cut it out, Eithne," said Fidelma, "put them out of their agony."

"All right, I'd do anything for you, twinnie," sang Eithne, handing the rest of the letters around the group.

Peace reigned for a few minutes, while everyone eagerly read their post.

"Well, what do you know," said Aileen. "The past pupils are having a special meeting next week in a hotel, to decide what they'll do for the 150th anniversary."

"A hotel?" said Judith without raising her eyes from the letter, "Why not at the school?"

Aileen turned over the page, and read on "It's because of the pageant," she explained. "They don't want to bother the school at such a time."

"More likely because of the hotel bar," snorted Josie. "It's much more fun deciding what to do about ghastly anniversaries when you've a glass of something in your hand."

"It's a lunch, and my mother doesn't drink," said Aileen in mock reproach, "and also Sr Gobnait will be there."

Josie laughed. "No one said it had to be an alcoholic drink, did they? Of course I was referring to the one and only *Jungle*." As she spoke, she winked.

"Listen gang," said Nuala excitedly. "This letter is from my brother. He thought that we would like to hear that a two-parter *Why Cases* will be on during the half term break. In it Weirdo Kelvin escapes from the detergent bottle and terrorises some university. He seems to like educational places, doesn't he?"

"Brilliant!" said Josie, "but it's weeks to half term. How will we last, how will we live till then?"

"Let's do another dare," suggested Aileen. "It's your turn, Nuala. What about it?"

"I couldn't possibly do one until the pageant is over, not to mention this special history project," said Nuala. "But once the pageant is over, Deirdre and I will do something, won't we Dee?"

"Definitely," agreed Deirdre. "Have you any ideas, Nuala?"

"I have, but I don't know if it's even possible to do it. I haven't worked it out yet," said Nuala mysteriously.

"How I wish we could see the *Why Cases* this week," said Aileen. "The *Rodent that Ratted* sounds brilliant."

Nuala looked down through the branches at the river flowing past below. "Who needs the *Why Cases*?" she said in a mysterious, far away voice. "When we have deep, deep down in the mud of the Boyne, the *Fearuisce*. Every hundred years exactly, its enormous bulging shapeless mass, with a salmon-like head and a tail like an eel, slithers out of the slime and across the countryside. Everywhere its grotesque shadow falls, be it on a person, place or even a castle, that object after one terrible cry, starts to shrink and goes on shrinking until it is only two inches high, or should I say three centimetres high."

"When did it last appear?" asked Aileen greatly amused.

"I can't remember offhand," said Nuala looking thoughtfully into the distance. "Could have been 1898 or maybe 1899, no, of course it was 1896."

"Why? Why? Why?" said Aileen dramatically.

"There's the bell for tea," interrupted Eithne, starting to move down the tree. "You can tell us the rest of the story tonight, Nuala."

Nuala held up her hand, "Wait, there may be no tonight," she said ghoulishly. "Fearuisce is stirring already – see?"

She pointed to the middle of the river which was unusually turbulent, with circles of waves radiating out from a dark point there. As they looked, a dark pointed head rose slowly out of the water before vanishing, leaving a trail of bubbles behind it.

"Come on, girls," said Josie. "Let's go. I want my tea before Nuala's friend throws his shadow on St B's, and the beans and chips shrink to nothing. I'm hungry."

"Laugh while you can," said Nuala cheerfully, following them down Barney and jumping lightly to the ground. "But don't say I didn't warn you. Remember, I won't take any stick from you when you are all running around beside the Boyne, only three centimetres high."

As they were coming out of study much later

that evening, Nuala asked Judith to go with her to the museum, as she wanted to ask Miss Ryan about old maps of the interior of the castle. When they arrived at the museum, Miss Ryan was only too happy to look through the maps there for Nuala.

"Here's one, about a hundred years old," she said carefully unfolding a large brownish piece of paper and spreading it out on the table in front of them. Warning them to be careful, she went off to attend to something else. Nuala studied the map for a while, then she pointed excitedly to a place on it which had "Library" written on it in faded pointed handwriting.

"It's exactly where we found it!" she cried. "Just beside the present library, which seems to be described as something's study."

Judith peered down at the faded lettering. "It looks like 'head . . . ' and a faded 's'." she said "Could it have been the headmistress's study in those days?"

"I guess you're right," said Nuala. "It couldn't have been much fun for the girls having the head's study just beside the library, could it?"

"No, but why are you so interested in the old library anyway?" asked Judith.

"Remember your idea that an old library full of books would be quite a good place to search for the missing list of prizewinners?"

"Oh yes," said Judith. "But there are millions of

books there, we'd never get finished searching through them."

Nuala carefully folded up the precious map and took it over to the teacher.

"Was it any help?" asked Miss Ryan.

"It was indeed, I found exactly what I was looking for," said Nuala. "Thank you, Miss Ryan. Is it possible for us to get into the old library?"

The teacher looked thoughtful. "I suppose you could get permission to go into it, but there's nothing to see there now," she said.

"Nothing?" said Nuala in a surprised voice. "What ever happened – there must have been thousands of books there?"

"Very true, but they were all removed to the present library. The old one was very small, you know. I don't think it is used for anything now," replied Miss Ryan. "Why are you so interested in it?"

"I just wondered about the missing prizewinners' list," said Nuala feeling very disappointed.

"No, it is definitely not there. That place is empty. The list must have been destroyed years ago, probably by accident. It's a pity, but it can't be helped," said Miss Ryan, smiling sympathetically at them. "I know how you feel. I'd love to find out who the missing winner of the *Merry Gold Medal* was too."

"It's more than that," said Nuala. "We are doing

our project as an investigation into the missing name. It won't be any good if we don't solve the mystery, it would just feel like a waste of time to me."

"I see," said Miss Ryan smiling again. "Are you by any chance trying to live out a real life *Why Case*?"

"I hadn't thought of it like that," said Nuala. "Now that you mention it, I think it's a brilliant idea!"

"You'll have to be Wolf Damper then," laughed Judith. "I know I'd be better as Dr Tully, writing in at the end of the project *'The best is yet to come'*."

They left the museum then and walked silently back towards the common room.

"They certainly cleared that library very quickly," said Nuala in a dejected voice. "I had great hopes of finding the list there; it seemed the right place somehow."

"Would you consider the top room of the tower?" suggested Judith, trying to be helpful. "That wardrobe we hid in last night, and those presses. You never know what we might find in them."

"The old wardrobe . . . " said Nuala slowly. "It's unlikely, but we can't afford to pass up anything. We won't go now, it's not a good time."

"We still have the key, what's stopping us going

up tomorrow after dinner? Remember it's Saturday and we've a free period then," Judith pointed out.

"Why not?" said Nuala cheering up at the thought. "But don't tell anyone, we would be better on our own."

"Right," said Judith. "It's a date. Promise you won't open any old detergent bottles we might find lying around there, all the same."

"I promise," laughed Nuala. "Imagine, Miss Ryan must be a follower of the *Why Cases* too. I'd never have guessed, would you?"

"Why not?" said Judith broad-mindedly. "Teachers are only human after all . . . I think."

On the following afternoon, when no one was watching them, Nuala and Judith quietly went up to their bedroom. It was the work of a moment to unlock the door, then they quickly ran up the stone staircase to the top room of the east tower.

"It looks so peaceful, doesn't it?" said Nuala looking at the sun shining brightly through the window, and on the dust which lay thickly on everything. "It's hard to believe that witches actually held covens here, it seems so innocent in the daylight."

"Last night everything was so different," said Judith. "Look, there are the velvet cushions I told you about, Nuala. Aren't they brilliant? And there are the candles on that wooden box there."

Nuala looked at them. "The witches do themselves well, don't they?" she said as she walked over to the presses and started rooting around in them.

"Here's the wardrobe," said Judith "It's pretty grotty, isn't it? It looked better in the dark."

Nuala went over and helped Judith search the wardrobe, which didn't take long.

"A couple of chewed pencils, one torn glove, three dog-eared pages, and an elastic band. That's the sum total," said Nuala looking at their findings five minutes later.

"Not to mention a load of dust all over us," said Judith ruefully, rubbing her sleeve. "I didn't really expect to find it here."

Nuala nodded absently as she stood looking out the window. "What a fabulous view there is from this window. The river, the fields, the trees," said Nuala, "plus the brand new fire escape steps."

Judith joined her at the window and looked at the metal steps leading down to the garden. "Wouldn't it be fun to go down those steps one night?" she said. "For a dare, of course."

"Some dare," said Nuala. "Maybe we could all go as a group dare. We'll put it to the others after the pageant."

"Was that the idea you had for Deirdre and yourself? I think it would be brilliant!"

"No, my idea was quite a different one. We'd

have to pick a night when the witches were safely out of the way though."

"There's always a catch when I think of something," complained Judith.

"Cheer up Ju," replied Nuala, as they ran back down the stone stairs to Annie's Pocket "We'll find a way to beat those witches. Trust us *Banshees*!"

15

Nuala Plans a Dare

"Oh Holy Patrick, you lit the flame, that Pascal flame, which overcame our darkness on the hill of Slane."

"You brought to us the light of Christ," Nuala sang. Her voice soared over the serried ranks of an audience totally absorbed, on this, the first night of the pageant *Spirit of St Brigid's*. The hall was packed not only with visitors but with the whole school, both staff and girls.

Under the cover of the enthusiastic applause which broke out when Nuala had finished her song, Clementine Vallely rose from her place among the sixth years at the back row. Nobody noticed her quietly leave by one of the doors in the rear of the hall. Making her way swiftly along the silent corridors, she soon reached the main office of the school, which was empty.

Once inside, she carefully closed the door, then went straight to a cabinet in which she knew the school reports were filed. Her objective was to find out how she had fared in the previous week's exams; her mother had rung that morning to say that she would be attending the parent-teacher meeting the following week.

It didn't take long to find the appropriate file and discover to her relief that, while her results were certainly not brilliant, they weren't a disaster either.

Feeling quite cheerful she replaced the file, nearly catching her finger in the lock on the drawer as she did so. Then, first peeping out of the door of the room to satisfy herself that the way was clear, she hastened back to join her classmates in the hall.

Slipping unobtrusively back into her place between June and Kelly she was pleased to find that she was in time for the final scenes of the pageant.

When the curtain fell for the last time, Clem joined in enthusiastically with the clapping and cheering, blissfully unaware that she had dropped her precious moonstone ring while closing the drawer of the filing cabinet in the school office. When the applause had died down a smiling Sr Gobnait rose to congratulate the producer Mrs Cuddy, the cast and everyone connected with the production of the pageant. Nuala, standing on the stage with all the other performers, longed to tear off her most uncomfortable red wig and change out of the long draperies she had to wear for the pageant.

Sr Gobnait had just finished saying that, though it would be invidious to pick out any one performer for special mention, as they all had been excellent, she had to praise Eilís Dunne's dancing, which she would describe as inspired.

At this point, Nuala felt she couldn't stick the discomfort of her costume any longer, so she backed slowly out of sight and went to the green room where she changed rapidly into her uniform again, returning before the head nun had finished her speech.

"I'll be in Dublin next Friday for the past pupils' luncheon meeting," Sr Gobnait was saying as Nuala quietly rejoined the cast on the stage, "but don't worry, you won't be deprived of my weekly pep talk. I know how much you would miss it, so I will have recorded it by tomorrow. Sr Joan will put it on the intercom at its usual time, twelve midday after the Angelus."

As Nuala joined in the general laughter which greeted this remark, a memory of something Aileen had said once about a *Banshee* dare, surfaced in Nuala's mind, making her think, *That's it. I've got my chance handed to me now!*

There was a general exodus from the hall soon afterwards, the girls going off to school supper, while parents and guests were taken to the parlour where they were served refreshments. Naturally, the *Spirit of St Brigid's* was the main topic of conversation, with unlimited praise being heaped on Eilís for her wonderful dancing performance.

Later that evening the jubilant Wiccans held a special meeting in their bedroom. "The knotted cord spell worked like a charm," said a flushed and excited Eilís happily. "I'm sorry I ever doubted it, Clem."

"It must be true," said Kelly. "You should have heard what the people were saying about you, Eilís."

"Let's have another meeting and try a spell that would improve my Maths," said June, sighing deeply. "Miss Lawless was very scathing about my work today."

"What about it, Clem?" asked Eilís.

"Why not? There's a full moon coming soon. We could do something special on that occasion," replied a gracious Clem, who was in very good spirits. "I must consult my charts, of course."

"Where's your ring?" June asked suddenly. "I thought you always wore it?"

Clem looked at her hand and gave a wild shriek, "My ring, my precious moonstone!" she cried. "What could have happened to it? where could I have lost it?"

"Think Clem," said Kelly. "When do you remember having it last?"

Clem tried to calm herself. "Let me think. I know I had it after dinner," she replied, looking worried. "I can't remember after that."

"Don't worry," said Eilís soothingly. "You must have lost it in the hall; we'll all go over there now and help you look for it. It's bound to be there."

"Good idea. Come on June," said Kelly pushing her towards the door. Clem could only throw Eilís a grateful glance as she followed them out. Poor Clem, thought Eilís, she is really worried about her moonstone ring.

While the Wiccans were searching everywhere in the hall for the ring, Nuala, having waved goodbye to her parents, was surprised to find Judith hanging around outside the castle waiting for her.

"Hi Ju, what's up? You look as if you've seen a ghost," said Nuala cheerfully as Judith joined her.

"Stop messing around, Nuala," replied Judith impatiently. "I want to tell you something very interesting without the whole place hearing me."

"Let's walk slowly to the common room then," said Nuala, wondering what Judith was being so secretive about.

"I was just passing the concert hall a few minutes ago and I could hear voices coming from it," said Judith. "Then, to my surprise the door opened and who do you think came out of it, but the girl from the library! When she saw me, she laughed and said, 'It's only a few sixth years looking for a lost ring'. Then she asked me how were we getting on in our search for the list of prizewinners."

"How did she know we were looking for that list?" asked Nuala increduously.

"Everybody knows we're looking for that list," replied Judith impatiently. "The thing is that this girl has promised to help us to find it!"

"Brilliant!" cried Nuala. "Did she say how?"

"Not really," replied Judith. "But she said she knew something that might be a help to us; she'd let us know later. She really is a very nice person, so friendly and pleasant. I never thought of asking her what her name is."

"I don't suppose you could," said Nuala. "It would be a bit cheeky to a sixth year. That reminds me, we must have a *Banshee* meeting. I've just had the most brilliant idea for a dare for next Friday."

"Good stuff, as Aileen would say," replied Judith. "But how will you manage it with two more performances of *Spirit of St Brigid's* to do and all the fuss that goes with them?"

"No probs," said Nuala cheerfully. "Wednesday will be the final night of the show. That will give me the whole of Thursday to finalise our plans. After all that holy singing, I feel the need to do something daring."

Judith laughed. "You sing so well too. Anyway let's have the meeting soon – as I want to hear your idea."

"How about after lights out tonight, will that be soon enough for you?" replied Nuala promptly.

"It's nearly that time already," said Judith. "I think I can wait till then!"

When the Banshees heard what Nuala's dare consisted of, at the meeting that night they voted unanimously that she should do it herself. Deirdre, having drawn her name out of the bag, would be her assistant.

So it was that three mornings later Nuala was awakened by the sound of a cock crowing followed by a precise voice saying, "5:35 am". As she stretched out her hand automatically to turn the talking watch off, realisation came to her that it was the Friday morning chosen for the most outrageous dare so far attempted by the club.

Groaning slightly, she dragged herself out of bed and pulled on a tracksuit and runners. Then, picking up her rucksack, she went off to rouse Deirdre, the co-darer, from her slumbers.

As it happened Deirdre was ready and waiting for her, so they didn't delay. As the pale morning light deepened and spread over the countryside the two *Banshees* left Annie's Pocket and sped on their way down to the school office. They were nearly there when Nuala broke the silence.

"I wish we didn't have to go through the big dormitory every time we want to leave our room," she grumbled in a low voice. "Passing through it in the early morning with everyone asleep gives me the creeps for some reason."

Deirdre nodded. "I know how you feel, I hate it too," she said.

Once inside the office Nuala became very business-like. Opening her rucksack she took several items from it, including a Walkman, a pen, a sheet of paper and a pair of gloves. Then, putting on the gloves, she went over to the intercom and removed the tape from the tape recorder connected to the microphone there.

Placing the tape in her Walkman, she pressed a button and Sr Gobnait's familiar voice could be heard calling for everyone's attention, which made Deirdre giggle quite a bit.

"I'm going to write down her speech and then listen to her voice a few more times so as to catch every inflection," said Nuala, grinning at the expression on Deirdre's face.

"I'll go out and keep watch as planned," said Deirdre. "I'll have hysterics if I stay in here with you. Remember you don't have that much time."

"I know," said Nuala. "But it's got to be right or it won't work. Just give me a shout when the time is up."

So Deirdre went out to keep watch on the corridors and stairs, while Nuala hastily wrote down Sr Gobnait's message, then ran the tape over and over again until she felt that she could reproduce the nun's voice accurately. She had just finished recording the amended talk on the tape, when the door opened and a worried looking Deirdre peeped in.

"Nuala," she whispered urgently. "It's getting terribly late, we need to go now."

Nuala looked up from her task. "I'm nearly finished Deirdre, you go along, I'll be right behind you," she said.

"Are you sure?" asked Deirdre, feeling relieved as it was now ten past six.

"Perfectly. You head off, I'd prefer it," replied Nuala, shoving her things rapidly back into the rucksack. Then she put the tape back into the recorder, beside the microphone. As she was checking the room to make sure that everything was as she had found it, the door opened again. Nuala, turning around, was amazed to see the girl from the library there, closing the door gently behind her.

"Come quickly," said the girl. "Sr Gobnait is walking down the stairs, she'll catch you if you go out that door."

As she spoke, she took a key from the row on the wall and went behind the filing cabinets, saying as she did so, "I'll let you out this door Nuala. It's not used much nowadays. Come quickly."

Nuala was too stunned to say anything, just grabbed her rucksack and meekly followed the girl. When the door was locked behind them again, the girl smiled at Nuala and said, "Go down that way there. It will bring you to the rear of the chapel, you should find it easy to get back to your dormitory then."

"How can I thank you?" stammered Nuala. "How did you know I was even there?"

The girl smiled her usual friendly smile and said, "Shush, it was nothing, just go quickly."

Nuala walked away, her mind a riot of confusing thoughts. She turned once, the girl waved, and Nuala heard a whisper that floated on the air towards her, it sounded very like *Alter Ipse Amicus*, but she couldn't be sure. She slipped back into her bed, as it was only about six-thirty, and to her surprise she fell asleep at once.

The *Banshee* club could hardly sit still at history class that Friday morning, with two of its members very tired after their early start, not to mention the certain tension Nuala was experiencing, as the time approached for Sr Gobnait's speech. Nuala and Deirdre appeared to be listening intently to Miss Ryan explaining to the class about the divisions in Europe in 1945 after the end of World War 2. In reality they were counting the minutes to midday. At last the Angelus rang. After it was recited, the intercom gave its characteristic crackle.

"Could I have everybody's attention please," came the familiar voice of Sr Gobnait. "As a reward for all the hard work everyone has put into the highly successful *Spirit of St Brigid's*, I have decided to give the school the rest of the day off. Also, there will be a showing of the film *Jumanji* in the gymnasium tonight. Enjoy your treats, and make the most of this splendid weather while it lasts."

There was silence for a minute, then everyone was cheering, clapping and even dancing around the classroom.

"Three cheers for Sr Gobnait!" called Grainne. Everyone joined in with enthusiasm.

Miss Ryan smiled as she gathered up her books, Then she called them to order. "I understand your excitement, but you must sit down and keep quiet for the few minutes that are left before the bell rings. I'm just as pleased as you are at this unexpected treat, but see how calm I am."

Laughing, they sat down again quietly in their places.

"Did the teachers really not know about the half day?" asked Gwendoline.

"I didn't anyway," replied Miss Ryan. "Not that I'm complaining, but it is very unlike Sr Gobnait to spring it on us like this."

The bell rang then, to Nuala's great relief.

16

The Murrays make a Stand

"Nuala, you were brilliant!" said Aileen, climbing up onto her special place in their favorite beech tree where Nuala was already sitting staring thoughtfully across the river. "I really thought you were Sr Gobnait herself!"

Nuala turned and smiled absently at her. "Thanks Aileen, I nearly believed it myself. I only hope she doesn't find out. I'll be expelled at least."

"How much of it was you?" Aileen asked eagerly, brushing aside any thought of Nuala being caught.

"Well, it was all me, but I suppose you mean what did I add in? Only the half day," replied Nuala.

"'Only the half day', I like that," chuckled Aileen. "'Only the half day'," she repeated, chuckling as Judith and Josie now appeared on the scene.

"Aren't we the lucky ones – dear Sr Gobnait

giving us a half day!" said Josie, "in such splendid weather too, ha, ha, ha."

"What's the matter Nuala?" Judith asked. "You don't seem yourself."

"Merely tired. Getting up at 5:35 am is not what I'm used to," said Nuala. "I was also worried that I might not come across well," she added.

"You needn't worry about that, you took everyone in."

"Judith, we must find out the name of that girl in the library. I looked at the sixth year table during dinner and I couldn't see her," said Nuala quietly.

"I know, it's strange isn't it; I'll ask Eithne to find out for us. If anyone can, she will."

"Good idea, Judith, but don't tell anyone about her rescuing me this morning. Promise."

"Certainly. It's an extraordinary tale all the same. How did she know you were in the office, for instance?" said Judith.

"What are two whispering about?" asked Josie.

"I'm really looking forward to seeing *Jumanji*," said Judith quickly changing the subject.

"Not to mention the special tea," said Josie gaily. "I only wish these 150th anniversaries would come around more often."

"Where are the others?" asked Nuala, grinning sympathetically at her.

"Well, the Murrays are at badminton and Ciara and Deirdre are playing poker with Monica and

Gwendoline," said Josie. "Most people are lying around. I wanted a game of hockey, but everyone said that it was too hot."

"So it is," said Judith. "Much too hot. The weather will break soon, Josie, and then you'll get all the hockey you want."

"Half term is only about a week away," said Nuala dreamily. "Then we'll be able to watch Wolf Damper as he catches Weirdo Kelvin yet again. Remember, he escapes from his detergent bottle and terrorises some university."

"Good stuff," said Aileen. "Oh, the bliss of lying late in bed in the mornings and watching the *Why Cases* in your own home."

"Oh, I don't know, there's something special about seeing them at religion class," laughed Josie. "I often wonder what that video *From Here to Maturity* was all about."

"Don't, Josie," said Aileen. "Someone might hear you. I still don't know how Miss Connolly never discovered the switch."

Some hours later, while the whole school was happily engaged in watching the film *Jumanji*, Sr Gobnait returned from her trip to Dublin. Anxious to hear how things had gone in her absence, she went in search of Sr Joan, who happened to be in the office at that time.

After a cordial greeting and a blow by blow description of the past pupils' lunch meeting, Sr

Gobnait enquired how the day had gone for St Brigid's.

"Very well indeed," replied Sr Joan. "They all enjoyed your treats, but why didn't you tell me about the half day?"

"What half day?" asked the puzzled Sr Gobnait.

"The one you gave the school," explained Sr Joan patiently, turning on the tape recorder.

A confounded Sr Gobnait listened intently, as the head girl's voice could be heard reading out a list of names.

"Oh dear," said Sr Joan. "I'd forgotten that I had taped over your speech. Anyway, take my word for it, you gave the school a half day. I heard it myself."

"It's very strange. I know it was late last night when I checked it, but I have no memory of ever mentioning a half day on that tape," said Sr Gobnait.

"We thought it was strange too," said Sr Joan. "It's just as well we're not superstitious."

"That reminds me," said Sr Gobnait, picking up her bags and preparing to leave, "Miss Connolly came to me this morning about something that has been puzzling her. Apparently, as she was returning to the castle late one evening, she noticed a light, or lights, flickering in the Religion room. Even though she went straight up there as soon as she came in, she was surprised to find the room in darkness and even locked. I think we had better keep a special watch on the girls, I don't like mysteries."

As she spoke, something lying on the floor between two of the presses caught her eye. She bent down and picked it up. "Why it's a ring, with a pretty moonstone," she said, handing the ring to Sr Joan. "I wonder who it belongs to and how it got there?"

Sr Joan looked at the moonstone ring. "I don't think I've ever seen it before," she said smiling. "Another mystery, would you say?"

"Put a notice on the board," said Sr Gobnait briskly. "When the owner turns up, you never know, we might get a clue or two from them."

Sr Joan sat down to write out the notice, and Sr Gobnait turned to leave the room. As she was about to open the door, she called over to the other nun, "Don't leave that ring lying around here, put it away somewhere safe."

The film *Jumanji* was a great success. As they all trooped up the stairs to bed that night, Gwendoline confided to her friend Monica that she was glad that she had never played a game where such terrible things could happen.

"All those monsters," she said, shuddering.

"Oh, I don't know," replied Monica. "It could be fun too. School gets so deadly boring at times."

"Very true, but half term starts next Friday, thank goodness," said Gwendoline consolingly.

Fidelma, who was just in front of them, nudged her cousin Judith, saying in a significant voice, "I think the game of dares is great fun, don't you Judith?"

Her cousin laughed. "Absolutely, especially as soon as the dare is finished and I'm safely in bed again," she replied.

"What's the game of dares about?" asked Monica, who always was curious about things. "I don't think I've ever heard of it."

"It's when somebody dares you to do something exciting, and even dangerous," replied Fidelma, impervious to the warning looks Judith was giving her. "For example, this is how you play it. I dare you to go down to Sr Gobnait and tell her that the Department of Education is putting the *Why Cases* on the Junior Cert, and that you've just heard this on the TV. Consequently, you are asking her permission to watch the programme every week so that you'll get an A1 in the exam."

Monica and Gwendoline laughed jeeringly at her. "That's not a dare, that's lunacy," said Monica.

"You think so? That's what makes the game so exciting," replied Fidelma smugly.

To Judith's relief, Eithne, pushing her way through the other girls, now joined them.

"Do you realise that the sixth year half term starts on Thursday, the day before we go home?" she said, giving Fidelma a knowing look.

"Just what the doctor ordered," replied Fidelma enigmatically. "We'd better get organised then."

"What are you talking about?" asked a mystified Judith.

"Wait and see," said Eithne as they went in through the dormitory door. "We'll tell you all about it tomorrow night."

"I'd better warn the others," said Judith sarcastically.

"Good idea," whispered Eithne. "Just *Banshees,* remember."

As it happened, at religion class the following day the main theme was the story of Moses leading the Israelites out of the bondage of Egypt and into freedom. Most of the class were fascinated by this tale, no one more so than the Murray twins.

That night just before lights out, the door of Annie's Pocket opened quietly and the two Murrays came stealthily in. Closing the door behind them, they walked into the room and announced,

"We want to hold a special *Banshee* meeting."

"Oh no!" said Ciara. "I'm in bed and I don't want to get out again."

So they all gathered in Ciara's cubicle to listen to the twins.

"What's all this about?" asked Judith crossly. She had played several strenuous games of badminton that afternoon and was anxious to get into her own bed as soon as possible.

"Keep your hair on," replied Fidelma.

"We've got a legitimate grievance," said Eithne dramatically. "I'm Moses, and have come to liberate the Murrays from the tyranny of you six. You've done all the dares and have never given us a chance to do even one."

"What dare do you want to do?" asked a puzzled Nuala. "Most people would rather not do dares; certainly no one will stop you doing one."

"We have this brilliant idea for a dare for next Thursday," said Eithne "Because the next day will be half term and we'll have a whole week off to recover."

"What's the dare?" asked Josie.

"We thought it would be cool to go down the fire escape from the top room and then through the wood to Barney and hold a meeting there in the moonlight."

"How do you know that it's going to be a moonlit night?" asked Deirdre, while Ciara shrank back in horror against her pillows.

"Of course there'll be moonlight," said Fidelma impatiently. "Every night this week I've looked out the dorm window and the place is simply flooded with it. Anyway, it will be even more spooky and frightening if there isn't any."

"I've just remembered the sixth years," said Judith. "They might catch us, or even worse, lock us out."

"Don't worry," said Eithne, brushing aside her objection. "They'll all be gone home hours before that. That's why I picked Thursday for the dare."

"Right," said Nuala. "Let's vote. All in favor say aye."

Everyone said aye, except Ciara who cried "Oh no, what a ghastly dare!"

"Don't worry," said Nuala kindly. "You don't have to come. Just stay in bed, we don't mind."

"I'll come," replied Ciara instantly. She didn't want to stay behind on her own. Anyway, she just knew that if anyone came in and found them gone, she's be blamed for everything.

"What happens when we reach Barney and sit there shivering in the moonlight?" asked Judith.

"Ha!" said Eithne. "That's where Fidelma and I come in. You six go out on your own and we'll come along after you and do what we intend doing. It will be a surprise dare."

"Good stuff," said Aileen. "I love surprises."

Then the twins slipped away as quietly as they had come and the others climbed back into their beds.

Meanwhile, in the room below them, a jubilant Clem was telling her friends that her precious moonstone ring had turned up.

"That's brilliant," said June. "I'm really glad. Now we can have that meeting you promised to help me with my Maths, remember."

"No problem," replied Clem happily. "First I must consult my charts and pick the best night, preferably one with a full moon. Is that all right?"

Eilís and Kelly raised no objections to this, and it was agreed between them that they would all go down to the garden and do their magic spell there on whatever night Clem might select for the next Wiccan meeting.

Back at the office, Sr Gobnait and Sr Joan were having a quiet consultation about the owner of the ring, Clementine Vallely.

"She said she must have dropped it when she was in here yesterday looking for post," explained Sr Joan.

"I wonder," said Sr Gobnait. "However, I don't want to make any false allegations. Everyone is innocent until proved guilty."

Sr Joan looked at her thoughtfully. "Somehow I don't think Clem or her friends have the wit to do anything very daring," she said.

"We'll keep a good eye on them all the same," said the senior nun. "Clementine Vallely got into a lot of trouble in her last school, I'm told."

17

Well Told by Moonlight

"Fidelma was quite wrong about the moonlight, wasn't she?" said Judith, who was standing at the open window of the top room in the tower. It was the following Thursday night and the *Banshees* were on their way out to the giant beech tree, to await the surprise promised by the Murrays.

"She certainly was," agreed Ciara from behind her. "There is no moonlight at all, just clouds, and a nasty grey mist over everything."

Nuala appeared at the top of the metal fire escape ladder. "What's keeping you lot?" she asked in a low voice. "Come on. It's a perfect night, so calm and still. Even the mist has a strange luminous quality about it."

"What she means is that it's spooky and exciting," explained Aileen. "Especially as it's now the witching hour and anything can happen."

"Don't!" cried Ciara, wincing. "Thank goodness the witches have gone home anyway."

Josie joined them at this point and they all followed Nuala quietly down the ladder and into the castle garden. Even the mist seemed thinner when they left the castle behind and started walking towards the wood. It also became brighter, especially as the trees had shed so many of their leaves, and soon they were climbing Barney and sitting on their usual branches there. The deep silence of the night was only broken by the occasional rustle of a leaf falling from the trees around them.

"It's chilly, isn't it?" said Nuala cheerfully, as she shone her torch around the trees. "Just as well we put on warm tracksuits, isn't it?"

"What's keeping them?" said Josie impatiently. "This isn't my idea of fun. I'd much prefer to be in my bed."

"Me too," said Deirdre.

Just then, something seemed to pass through the trees and settle on one of the branches above them. Nuala directed her torch idly at the bough.

"Look, oh look," she whispered. "Just above us, there."

Immediately all eyes turned to look, and they were rewarded by the sight of a pair of large eyes gleaming down at them.

"Why, it's a barn owl," said Judith in delight "Isn't it beautiful!"

Giving a mournful hoot, the owl silently took off, moving slowly through the trees.

"Which twin was that?" joked Aileen, as they watched it fly away.

"I don't know," laughed Josie. "But it was a nice surprise."

Judith suddenly cried out, "There you are at last, what a fright you gave me."

Hearing this, the others turned towards Judith where they were surprised to see two masked figures, complete with long fair wigs, sitting on the branch next to her.

Aileen gave a sigh of relief. "The Murrays have turned up!" she cried. "What kept you?"

"I'm sorry we're late," replied one of the newcomers. "See, I've brought a friend who is going to tell you a story."

"Good stuff," said Aileen. "Fidelma's stories are always worth listening to."

"Is it one of your Collier the robber stories?" asked Deirdre, as they were particular favourites of hers.

The first girl shook her head.

"This is a story about jealousy, and how it affected one girl's life," said the second girl, speaking in low clear tones.

"First of all you must know that school life in the past wasn't as free and easy as it is today. Silence had to be observed all over the castle. Corridors, dormitories, the lot. The rules were strict, the holidays short and punishments severe.

"Towards the end of the last century two girls came to St Brigid's: Elizabeth, known affectionately as Lizzie, and the other was called Emer.

"Ambitious, hard working and very observant of the rules, the latter became a favorite of the nuns and teachers and especially of the headmistress, Sr Bernard. She achieved distinction in most things, becoming class captain early on in her career. Despite this, there was one thing which Emer coveted more than any other honour: The *Merry Gold Medal,* awarded annually to the girl whom the school voted as their nicest. But no matter how hard she tried, the prize always eluded her.

"Lizzie too, was hard working and successful, but unlike Emer didn't think that was everything in life. Consequently, she formed a secret society with other kindred spirits. Calling themselves the *Banshees,* this club was dedicated to friendship and fun.

"The members met regularly and challenged each other to carry out exciting dares. At this point in the story, one of them had thought up a new dare. So, masked and wearing their long cloaks, they met in the top room of the east tower, their usual venue on these occasions. None of them realised that Emer, who had been closely watching them for some time, had crept up to the top room behind them.

"On this occasion Lizzie herself had drawn the

dare, which challenged her to go into Sr Bernard's study and stand in the middle of the room and sing all eight verses of the school song out loud, not stopping for any reason whatsoever until she finished it. Also, to prove that she had completed this onerous feat, she was told to tear the day's date from the big calendar which stood on the headmistress's desk.

"Lizzie, in customary fashion, had gaily accepted her task, not realising that Emer had overheard every word that had passed between them, including the fact that Lizzie had planned to carry out the dare at seven pm on the following evening when the nuns would be at prayer. To do this she had also arranged to change music practice times with another girl to give her a reason for getting out of study at that time.

"The next morning started badly for Lizzie as she was late getting up. However, as she was running downstairs she met a nun, Sr Louise, who asked her to take a large packet of letters over to Sr Bernard's study.

"'Yes sister,' Lizzie managed to say breathlessly, before she went speeding on her way to the headmistress's study, feeling particularly hungry.

"Getting no reply to her respectful knock, she turned the handle of the study door and peeped nervously in. The room was empty. Closing the door carefully behind her, she proceeded across the room, depositing with relief her heavy bundle on Sr Bernard's desk.

"As usual, the study was in perfect order. Lizzie looked curiously around the bare austere room, with its shelves of neatly stacked books and papers, noticing especially the door in the back wall of the room, which was used exclusively by the head nun herself.

"Standing in the middle of the room, the big wooden desk was sparsely furnished, with just a large inkwell, several neatly aligned pens and a spotless blotter. To one side of them stood a white alabaster statue of an angel, whose large wings protected a frightened looking child. This was flanked on one side by a tall wooden stand on which hung a thick wad of white paper inscribed with the date of the day and month on it, and on the other side with a large vase of late roses.

"It was only when she saw the famous calendar that she remembered the *Banshees'* dare. Her face broke into a mischievous smile. "What luck!" she breathed "All I have to do is take today's date off of the calendar as proof that I've been here, that is after I've sung the school song."

"Standing up straight, she started singing loudly:

"*St Brigid's, St Brigid's, here we stand,*

"*Loyal to God, to you and to our native land . . .*

"Inwardly she was thankful that she had closed

the study door behind her, and at the same time she hoped that no one would come in and catch her there.

"She was lucky, no one disturbed her singing, even though she faithfully went through the whole eight verses, feeling an incredible idiot. That is, no one except Clement the cat, who had been sunning himself on the window sill, a favourite spot of his. He merely looked balefully in at her, then went back to sleep.

"When she had finished her task, she leant over the desk and gently ripped off the top leaf of the calendar, folded it in two and stuffed it in the pocket of her skirt.

"Chuckling to herself as she left the room, she decided not to tell anyone about her adventure but wait until after seven that evening and produce her proof. She decided that she would even go through the swapping of practice times with Rosa as agreed upon.

"Later that day, as they were in the cloakroom changing their shoes for break, Anne and Sarah demanded to know the reason why she had been so late for breakfast. Lizzie smiled mischievously at them.

"'Wouldn't you like to know?' she teased.

"'I would,' said Anne. 'You're up to something, Lizzie.'

"'I agree,' said Sarah. 'What were you doing?'

"Lizzie finished fastening her shoes, then she stood up. 'Nothing much,' she said vaguely. 'Actually, I was doing an errand for Sr Louise.'

"Before they could question her further, Rosa joined them, all excitement. 'Did you hear that not only is the winner of the *Merry Gold Medal* to be announced this evening, but,' here she paused for effect and looked importantly at them, 'It is rumoured that the winner is from our year! What do you think of that?'

"'How thrilling. I hope it's Lizzie,' said Anne quickly. 'I voted for her anyway.'

"'Me too,' said Rosa. 'She deserves it.'

"'Please girls, you're embarrassing me!' cried Lizzie, covering her face with her hands.

"'Oh Lizzie, let me be the first to congratulate you,' said a quiet voice from behind them.

"Lizzie spun around. There in front of her stood a tall thin girl dressed with excessive neatness and with a saintly look on her face.

"'Oh, it's you, Emer,' Lizzie said in a flat voice, very unlike her usual friendly tones. 'What are you congratulating me about?'

"Emer's eyes widened innocently. 'Haven't you heard then, or is it just modesty?' she replied sweetly. 'You're this year's winner of the *Merry Gold Medal*, I believe.'

"Rosa looked curiously at her. 'How did you find that out?' she asked brusquely. 'How can you be so sure?'

"Emer smiled again. 'I have ways of finding out things,' she replied gently. 'You'd be surprised at the amount of things that I know about you, Rosa.'

"'Pay no attention to her Rosa,' said Lizzie. 'Come on girls, let's go out for our walk, we've wasted enough time already.'

"The others hastened to follow her as she left the cloakroom. Emer watched them as they left, a strange expression on her face.

"'Do you think she does really know things about us?' asked Anne worriedly, as they walked around the garden.

"'I'd say she overheard Rosa and couldn't resist a stab at her.' replied Lizzie. 'Let's forget her now. It's October already, only two months to the Christmas holidays.'

"'She always reminds me of a cat with those green eyes," said Rosa. 'She certainly acts like one.'

"Lizzie laughed and said light-heartedly 'That's where she gets her information from, Clement, of course.'

"'I shouldn't be surprised,' agreed Rosa, grinning in spite of herself.

"Sr Bernard frowned in puzzlement at the anonymous letter in her hand, which read as follows:

"*I'm only doing my duty in reporting to you that a certain girl is planning to enter your study this evening at quarter to seven for an unlawful purpose. As proof that this is genuine, you will find today's page torn from your desk calendar. It will be in her possession.*

"As she stood irresolute, the school clock struck the quarter hour, galvanising her into action. Five minutes later, panting slightly, she reached the private door to her study just in time to hear a tremendous crash from within. Sr Bernard was no coward, she just lifted her lamp on high, threw open the study door and called out in a loud voice,

"'Stop at once, whoever you are. Stop, I say.'

"In the silence which followed, the nun looked around her study, aghast at the scene which met her eyes. Papers and books lay scattered around the floor, the statue of the angel, hanging drunkenly by a wing from the desk, gazed at the roses which lay in the center of a rapidly widening pool of water.

"As she picked her way through the chaos on her way to the main door of the room, she seethed with rage against the perpetrators of this outrage. Though she hadn't any hope of catching anyone, she opened the door and looked down the corridor. A little distance away she could see a girl walking away from her. In response to her call, the girl turned and came slowly back towards the nun.

"'What are you doing here at this time Elizabeth?' asked Sr Bernard, 'Surely you should be at study now.'

"A startled Lizzie blushed and stammered

hesitantly, 'I am on my way from the music room, Sister.'

"As the nun looked keenly at her, neither of them noticed a large black cat walk stealthily out of the study and sit down only inches behind Sr Bernard, where it proceeded to groom its ruffled fur.

"'Why did you leave the music room at this time? It's not seven o'clock yet,' asked the nun, rendered suspicious by Lizzie's manner.

"Before she could answer, Lizzie felt an enormous sneeze coming on, so she groped frantically for her pocket. As she pulled out her handkerchief, she was unaware that she had also pulled out a stiff piece of folded paper which, falling to the floor, came to land at Sr Bernard's feet.

"As Lizzie mopped her streaming eyes following her paroxysm of sneezing, she wasn't really surprised to see a pair of eyes like lamps gleaming at her from behind the nun, before Clement's vast bulk turned and vanished into the darkness.

"'Elizabeth, I can't believe it!' gasped Sr Bernard. 'And you this year's *Merry Gold Medal* winner too!'

"'Can't believe what, Sister?' asked a puzzled Lizzie.

"'Don't try to deny it, Elizabeth, I have the proof in my hand.' And with that the nun opened the piece of paper which she had picked up from the floor. Written on it was,

TUESDAY 31ST OCTOBER 1896
That one may smile and smile and be a villain.'
Hamlet

"Nothing that Lizzie could say would convince Sr Bernard of her innocence. The more she pleaded the more the nun thought badly of her. She wasn't punished except that Sr Bernard absolutely refused to give her the *Merry Gold Medal*, deliberately leaving the shield blank for that year. A cloud hung over her remaining time in St Brigid's causing her such great distress that she finally persuaded her parents to take her away from the school.

"I am telling you this because I cannot rest until this wrong is righted and her name engraved on the shield, as it should have been originally."

"What was Lizzie's second name?" called Nuala urgently. "How can you prove that this story is true?"

The moon which had been hiding behind clouds, at this point broke through, flooding the wood with light, momentarily dazzling the girls' eyes. When they could see again, their visitors had left Barney and were walking away through the trees.

As they watched the silhouettes fading into the darkness, a faint voice was borne back to them, "Find the missing list," it seemed to say.

"I don't know about you," said Deirdre firmly, "but I'm going back to Annie's Pocket this minute."

166

"Me too," agreed Ciara, following her down the tree.

As they were all approaching the castle again Josie pointed to two figures mounting up the fire escape to the top room.

"That was brilliant," said Aileen. "But where did the twins get that story from, I wonder?"

"It was interesting, but quite scary too," said Josie. "What do you think, Deirdre?"

"Definitely scary. I don't really think I understood the end though," replied Deirdre.

Nuala and Judith said nothing; they were both thinking desperately where the missing list could be, and whether it still existed anywhere.

The following morning Nuala was rudely awakened by Eithne shaking her vigorously.

"Wake up Nuala, wake up!" she was saying. "We have to go, Mum came unexpectedly early for us. I just want to explain about last night. Margaret Jones suddenly took sick and by the time Sr Joseph came and went, it was too late for us to do much. I'm really sorry. Goodbye."

"See you next week, goodbye," mumbled Nuala.

Nuala, who had been only half awake during this exchange, gave a puzzled look at Eithne's retreating back and fell back asleep again.

18

Lost and Found

Half term ended on Sunday and, as usual, all afternoon and early evening there was a buzz of chat and excitement through the castle, as the girls returned back from their break.

A little after six pm Kelly, laden with bags and books, pushed open the door of their bedroom in the tower, only to find that she appeared to be the first back that evening. However, subsequent investigation revealed June lying on her bed with earphones on, listening dreamily to a tape on her Walkman.

"Hi June," she said from the door of the cubicle. "What are you listening to?"

June looked up and turned off her Walkman. "Hi Kelly," she replied. "It's the latest sound track from the *Why Cases*. It's only just out and I couldn't wait to hear it."

"Wow, the *Why Cases*. I must borrow it from you. Wasn't the Rodent episode brilliant?" she said.

June nodded, then sat up, swinging her feet to the floor. "How did your holiday go?" she asked.

"Fine. I saw Clem in town one day. She was chatting up a tall fair guy at the time, so I didn't butt in."

"Was she? It was probably Gareth. Did you get much study done?" yawned June.

"Not really. I brought home a lot, but the week just flew. How about yourself?" asked Kelly.

June made a face. "I meant to do loads, but somehow I never got around to it. I haven't even changed yet. I hate getting back into uniform," she said.

Kelly laughed. "I know, it's a pain coming back to school again," she said sympathetically.

The door opened and Clem entered in her usual stately fashion. "Hi girls," she said in a voice unusually animated for her. "Did you hear about Eilís? She won't be back till Tuesday; she's got an audition for the Taylor school of dance and drama."

"You are not serious," gasped June. "Not *the* Taylor school, it's almost impossible to get an audition for a place there, I hear."

Clem threw her bags on her bed. Then, smiling complacently, she said proudly, "We all know who to thank for that, don't we? What about the spell of the knotted cords, for instance?"

For some reason Kelly, irritated by this remark,

169

replied brusquely, "She hasn't got the place there yet. I bet simply thousands are being auditioned anyway."

"Well, if that's your attitude," said Clem, "I won't bother doing anything for June. As it happens, by putting myself to a lot of bother I managed to acquire a special spell to help her with her Maths problem. Don't worry, I won't bother her, I'll just concentrate on my Karma instead." With that she went into her cubicle, banging the door loudly behind her.

Kelly and June exchanged glances. "I really must find out what this Karma thing is," said June, slipping her earphones on again and returning to the comfort of the *Why Cases* music.

Kelly, looking glum, went into her own cubicle and started her unpacking.

Meanwhile, above in Annie's Pocket, Nuala and Judith were discussing the story that Fidelma had told them out in Barney on the night of the dare.

"Now that Eithne and Fidelma won't be back for a week because of flu," Nuala was saying, "I won't be able to find out from them where they got that extraordinary tale from. Did they say anything to you?"

"No," replied Judith. "We didn't have time on the Friday we went home and I wasn't allowed see them before I came back, in case of infection, so I never heard any details at all."

"Pity. The whole thing is inexplicable," said Nuala. "It's so much easier for Damper and Tully, somebody else writes the script for them. Seriously though, we must find that list."

"I know," said Judith. "If only we had a clue where to look for it."

Aileen and Josie came in then.

"They must have got cold on the night of the dare. It was freezing out in those damp misty woods," said Josie, when Judith had told them the bad news about the twins.

"Lucky things," said Aileen grumpily. "I can't understand why we all didn't get 'flu. Come to think of it, they were wrapped up in thick cloaks too, not like us only in track suits."

"I'm glad I didn't get sick," said Nuala. "I'd hate to miss the special day off on Thursday."

"You mean the free day we are to spend in exactly the same way as they used to spend it a hundred years ago, when they didn't have half terms?" said Josie. "I'm looking forward to that too."

"I hope you won't be disappointed," said Aileen, who didn't seem to be in her usual good form.

Judith studied her closely. "I hope you're not getting the flu." she said.

"Pshaw," said Aileen rudely.

As it happened, the special day turned out to be a great success. It started with sixth years dressed in

171

a mad variety of costumes, going around the school waking everyone up with music and song. This was considered good fun, especially as they weren't called until nine am. When they arrived down to the refectory for an old fashioned breakfast of hot porridge, they found all the tables and chairs were upside down and they had to sit on the tables and eat from the chairs. The reason for this exercise was a bit obscure, but possibly it had some special significance for the girls who had been at St Brigid's one hundred years previously.

In the afternoon the school divided into two teams: one green, the other blue – which were the school colours – and then into groups of twenty-five. Each group had a choice of several ways of spending their time until the special dinner at six pm. This included shopping, sightseeing, playing games or even ice skating.

After a sumptuous banquet in the evening, a happy crowd gathered in the hall to be given instructions on how to play "Seek and Avoid", the wind-up event of the day.

"Seek and Avoid" was really meant to be played around the extensive school grounds, Sr Gobnait explained to them, but as the day had turned out to be extremely wet, this couldn't be done. However, the castle was enormous and on this auspicious occasion they were allowed to go all over it, even to places usually forbidden to the girls. The nuns and staff had all been warned to lock their rooms, so that the girls were free to go anywhere they pleased.

She then enunciated the principles of the game:

1) They would keep to their colors and groups of twenty-five.

2) The Blues would go off first to hide and after fifteen minutes a bell would ring and the Greens would go in search of them.

3) The objective was for the Blues to try and creep back to the hall without been caught or seen.

4) Obviously the objective for the Greens was to go out and catch them. Points would be given for catching sight of any rival group member.

5) The only absolute rule was that they must always move, hide and act, as a unit of twenty-five.

6) When all the Blues were back in the hall, or caught, then it would be the turn of the Greens to hide.

7) The game would go on until 10:30 pm.

8) Points would then be added and whichever color got the highest points would win a prize.

In answer to many voices, Sr Gobnait replied "Yes, of course the castle would be in complete darkness except for the stairs, but you can take torches."

After a certain amount of consultation, the blue groups set off to hide. Nuala, Gwendoline and

Monica found themselves in the same group, led by two sixth years, one of whom was Kelly Wallace. Nuala grinned to herself, remembering the episode on the stairs of the east tower, when the *Banshees* were waiting to hold a meeting there.

Even though the game hadn't sounded that good when Sr Gobnait had been describing it, once they started playing it, it turned out to be great fun. Moving as a unit of twenty-five was quite difficult, but it only added to the fun.

In the first game, Nuala's group had almost made it to the hall, when they had been sighted in the last few yards dash to it. In consequence, when the blues' turn came again, Kelly and the other leader, Joan, were determined not to be caught a second time.

They went much further into unknown territory this time, trying to find a new way back to the hall. It was when they were creeping quietly along a strange corridor that Kelly, counting her group, found two of the girls were missing. She directed Nuala to go back along the way and try and find them. The group would wait where they were for her return.

Nuala didn't have far to go before she found the missing pair. They were in a room strange to Nuala, but it looked like a sitting-room of some sort. As she came into the room and flashed her torch around she heard someone calling to her.

"Nuala, we're over here, come and see if you can help us."

Nuala hurried over, where to her amazement she saw Monica standing shining her torch on a large handsome bureau which Gwendoline was desperately trying to close.

"Oh Nuala," cried Gwendoline. "We looked in here for a minute and I saw this bureau, it's just like one my granny has. So I thought I'd show Monica the secret drawer in it, but now I can't close it."

"Is there anything in it?" asked Nuala.

"Not a thing, not even in the secret drawer," said Gwendoline, opening and closing the elaborately engraved lid again.

"Hold this torch," said Nuala. "I'll try, but I don't suppose it'll do any good."

She opened the lid and gently tried to close it, but she couldn't do anything with it. Then she opened it again and looked inside. It was completely empty as Gwendoline had said. She pressed her hand all along the inside of the lid but in vain. As she was about to shake her head, and advise them to leave and join the others, she felt something in behind the metal band which operated the lid. Holding her breath, she rooted behind the band. Yes there was something there. She pulled and pulled as carefully as possible. Suddenly a piece of paper appeared. Gently she moved it up and down and eased it out. Now the lid closed down without any bother.

"Oh Nuala, you genius," said Gwendoline gratefully.

Nuala thrust the piece of battered paper into her pocket and started for the door. "Come on," she said "We must join up with our group again."

As they hurried out the door of the room, Kelly Wallace and the rest of the group came up to them.

"Thank goodness," she cried. "Whatever kept you, Nuala? And you two, don't ever leave the group again!"

A chastened Gwendoline and Monica fervently apologised and promised to obey the rules from then on.

This time they were lucky and managed to reach the hall without being caught. At the end of the evening the blues won by two points. Sr Gobnait awarded the prize to the successful side. They found that it was a huge tin of sweets, enough to share with the losers.

As the tired but happy girls prepared for bed that night, they all agreed that free days of the past had a lot to recommend them.

The following morning when Nuala was dressing she noticed a piece of yellowish looking paper on the floor beside her bed. Picking it up, she was about to throw it automatically into a wastepaper basket, when something written on it caught her eye. It was the word "Merry" written in thin pointed handwriting. She recognised the piece of paper as the one that she had found the night before, and with trembling hands she unfolded it carefully.

When she had spread it out flat, she found that it was a list of names, half of them incomplete due to the paper having been torn at some stage in its history. But under the words *Merry Gold Medal 1896* was written clearly in a firm hand: *Elizabeth Bruder*.

19

June Makes a Decision

Miss Ryan stared in amazement at the piece of tattered paper which Nuala had just handed to her. "The missing prize list, is that what you said?" she gasped "I don't believe it!"

"I know, it's fantastic. But we're hoping you'll confirm it," said Nuala.

There was silence as the teacher gently smoothed out the yellowing crumpled edges of the jagged sheet of paper and looked carefully at the pointed handwriting on it. "It looks like the missing list, or at least part of it," she said at last. "One thing is clear; someone called Elizabeth Bruder won the *Merry Gold Medal of 1896*."

Nuala and Judith looked with delight at each other and then at the teacher.

"Where did you find it?" asked Miss Ryan.

So Nuala told her what had happened on the night of the special free day when she had gone to help Monica and Gwendoline close the lid of the old bureau.

"How exciting," said Miss Ryan. "I'd love to know the story behind the blank shield, wouldn't you?"

"We have some ideas about that too," replied Nuala in a cautious voice. "But we'd prefer not to tell anyone until we've got the whole story written down."

"I'll certainly look forward to reading it then," said Miss Ryan, smiling at them. "All the same, I'll show this list to Sr Gobnait. She will be pleased."

"Miss Ryan," said Judith earnestly. "Please don't tell anyone about the list, except of course Sr Gobnait. You see, Nuala and I want it to be a surprise for everyone."

"You know the sort of thing," agreed Nuala. "'The case of the shield without a name, an investigation carried out by two intrepid reporters'."

Miss Ryan laughed. "Don't worry, I'll bind Sr Gobnait to secrecy. At the rate you're going, I believe you'll be included in the past pupils' anthology for the 150th anniversary," she said.

Only that morning Sr Gobnait had announced to the school that the past pupils had decided to publish a book on the history of St Brigid's, adding that a competition would be held, and space would be allotted to any outstanding contributions from the pupils themselves, with the winning stories included in the volume.

"Marvellous," said Judith. "My mum and dad would be thrilled if we got into that book."

"So would mine," agreed Nuala.

"Well, you never know your luck," smiled the teacher. "We must get Elizabeth Bruder's name engraved on the shield anyway."

"We must photograph it first," said Nuala. "A before and after snap would be essential for our report."

"I'll be in the museum in the morning," said Miss Ryan helpfully. "You can photograph it then."

"Brilliant!" said Judith. "I'm glad I remembered to bring my camera back with me."

Having thanked the teacher, they left her and set off for the common room to join their friends who were relaxing there after an arduous day of lessons. On arrival, they discovered Grainne, the class captain, holding forth on the latest rumour circulating the school.

"It's definitely the ghost of Lady Marjorie Calfe, who threw herself from the top room of the east tower," she was saying dramatically. "We're being haunted!"

"Never heard of her," said Monica indifferently, who was one of a group sitting on the floor impatiently waiting for the soap *Together and Apart* to appear on the television. "What's she doing anyway?"

"Her ghost is haunting the castle," replied Grainne crossly.

"Not again," said Deirdre in a bored voice. "Do you remember the last time, and it was only a teacher messing around. Tell us something new for a change."

"What do you know about the ghost?" asked Aileen.

"Madeline Smith swears she saw strange lights in their dorm the other night again, the first time was just before half term. Then that kid in first year, Mary O'Reilly, says that a figure with long fair hair glided past her in a corridor one night, before vanishing into the religion room, which could have been the Calfe's sitting-room."

"You're not serious!" said Judith. "Did she get a look at the ghost's face, by any chance?"

"She was a bit vague about that, just mad staring eyes was all she could remember," replied Deirdre, who had obviously taken the ghost story to heart. "Miss Connolly told someone that she had seen strange lights darting around the religion room when she was returning to the castle late one evening. When she rushed upstairs and found it in darkness, it had a strange eerie feel to it."

"It sounds like a case for the *Why* team to me," said Aileen cheerfully. "Damper and Tully to the rescue of St Brigid's would be great."

"Sometimes, Aileen, your idea of humour borders on the asinine," snapped Grainne. "You

181

think you're smart, but I bet you'd be as scared as the rest of us if the ghost appeared in the common room one night."

"Of course I would," agreed Aileen. "But then, as I don't believe in ghosts, I don't think it's likely to happen either."

To everyone's relief the door of the common room opened and Josie came in all excitement. "Hi girls," she said "What's wrong, you all look as if you've seen something strange. Anyway, you should be down at the office. Sr Gobnait is doing a version of the Indian Rain dance of delight around the sixth years, especially Eilís Dunne."

"Come off it, Josie," said Judith. "What do you take us for – Sr Gobnait dancing!"

"It's true, honestly. Apparently Eilís has been offered a place in some fab dance school, beating about five hundred others in the process."

"Wow!" said Aileen, "She must be good."

"By the way," said Josie, handing Judith a large square envelope. "Here's some post for you."

Judith quickly opened the envelope, pulling out a large poster depicting the familiar features of Wolf Damper and Evadne Tully looking all keen and Why case-ish. "It's from Eithne," she said quickly skimming through the letter which accompanied it.

Unlike Grainne's ghost story, the poster soon had the attention of everyone in the common room.

"It's simply brilliant!" said Aileen "Where are you going to put it?"

"I don't know, the dorm I suppose," said Judith vaguely as she was engrossed in the letter. There was a chorus of disapproval from the girls at this. Everyone thought such a picture should grace the common room where the whole year could have the benefit of it. Judith good-naturedly agreed and several people at once started arguing over where it should go.

"Any news from the twins?" asked Nuala.

"They're both better, but won't be back until next week."

"Lucky things, having an extra week at home."

Judith looked around the room, then lowered her voice. "Remember we heard that Clem Vallely, one of those witches, was supposed to have been expelled from her last school because of her interest in Nature, or something? Eithne says it's all a fake. The truth is that she was messing around with her boyfriend and not studying, and her mum took her away and sent her here to work hard and do well in the Leaving."

"You don't say!" replied Nuala, much amused "Trust Eithne to have found it all out."

There was great merriment in Annie's Pocket that night when Aileen reminded them of Grainne's story of the haunting of St Brigid's.

"Did you ever hear of such nonsense," scoffed Ciara. "Why would any ghost want to haunt a school?"

"Oh, I don't know," said Nuala. "I liked the part about the mad staring eyes. Was that you, Aileen, do you think?"

Aileen grinned "Maybe, but appearing as darting lights in the religion room is really more my style."

Sometime later, when Eilís, flushed and starry eyed, was preparing for bed, June, who had been thinking hard, suddenly announced, "That settles it. If the knotted cords helped Eilís so much, you'll have to do a Maths spell for me. I need it desperately, Clem."

"Fine," said Clem. "Nothing easier. I'll study my charts and pick a suitable night with a full moon, if possible."

"Great. What do we have to do?" asked June, while the other two listened with interest.

"First we have to find a yew tree, then a holly tree, and finally an oak tree with ivy growing all over it. They all have to be fairly near to each other, so that at midnight we can cast the spell in a open space between them."

"That should be easy here, with a wood just beside the garden," replied June optimistically. "We can go down by the fire escape."

"That sounds good fun, but don't leave it too late, the nights are getting very chilly," said Kelly.

Eilís laughed happily. "We want June to get an A in Maths, not in pneumonia," she said gaily.

20

All's Well that Ends Well

Once June had made up her mind to use a Wiccan
spell in order to improve her performance at
mathematics, she became impatient with any delay
in carrying it through. Under such pressure, Clem
speedily discovered that the following Friday night
would fulfil the necessary conditions.

As she carefully explained to the sisterhood,
"June's birth sign is Libra, which means that the
lunar eclipse next Friday gives her leave to enjoy
life's simple pleasures. Now that her ruler, Venus, is
in the ascendant, she should go to it at once, before
Saturn or Pluto takes over, which would destroy
any chances of the spell being a success."

Put like that, they all agreed that it would be
madness not to cast the spell on the coming Friday.
Therefore, around eleven forty-five on the night in
question, if anyone had been watching, they would
have seen four figures slipping down the fire escape
in the East tower and vanishing into the woods
which lay beyond the castle garden.

As it happened, Sr Gobnait was also working late that night. Anxious to reduce the backlog of paperwork which had built up on her desk, she never noticed the time passing. The school clock striking one came as quite a surprise to her.

Pushing aside the form she was filling in, she got up and walked over to close the study window. As she leant forward to do this she saw the moon silently float out from behind a dark bank of clouds, throwing a silvery trail of light across the dark surface of the Boyne, as it flowed past the castle in its usual mysterious fashion. As she stood there admiring the sheen on the river, her eye was caught by another light in a place where there shouldn't have been any light at that time of night, namely the east tower.

Instantly alert, she took a key from her desk and set off in the direction of the tower. Arriving there, she unlocked the door and went swiftly up the stone stairs. She wasn't really surprised to find the door of the sixth years' bedroom wide open. Muttering grimly, "As I suspected, Clementine Vallely is involved in this," she continued on up the stairs.

Blissfully unaware of Nemesis stalking them, the four tired but satisfied Wiccans had just arrived back in the top room again, feeling very pleased with themselves. Everything had gone as planned. The trees were easily found and the spell enthusiastically chanted. Now they stood around their wooden box table watching June relight two of the candles which had gone out in their absence with an improvised taper made of stiff paper.

Suddenly they heard the heavy tread of someone walking up the stone staircase, approaching the door of the room.

"Blow out the candles and split," hissed Clem, leading the way to the fire escape. Kelly and Eilís swiftly blew out the candles, but June, losing her head flung away the lighted taper, which landed on a heap of dust sheets nearby.

They all scrambled out of the window on to the fire escape. Sr Gobnait threw open the door and marched into the room just in time to see Kelly silhouetted against the window, before she disappeared from sight down the metal ladder. The nun ran across to the window in hot pursuit of the wrongdoers, not realising that in the room behind her a spark from the taper had ignited the dust sheets. Within minutes, the fire was spreading rapidly, engulfing everything in its way across the room.

While this was going on upstairs, one flight below in Annie's Pocket Nuala was dreaming that she was taking part in a *Banshee* meeting. In the dream, the other members present were wearing long wigs and grey cloaks, but the eyes which glittered from behind their masks did not belong to

187

friends, but to strangers. A great fear came over her at this, and was intensified when the other Banshees pointed at her chanting in unison ,

"It's Nuala's turn to do the dare!"

"What dare?" she quavered from a dry throat.

"You must impersonate Sr Gobnait for a day. Lock her up in her room and then take her place in the school," came the chant in squeaky high pitched voices.

"I . . . I couldn't, it's impossible," she croaked.

The air grew thick and smoky. The other *Banshees* got up and marched menacingly towards her. "Do the dare or pay the fine," they shouted at her.

Her throat felt constricted, but she managed to gasp out, "What's the fine?"

"Throw yourself from the east tower," was the horrific answer she received.

She was walking blindly towards the window when a clear sweet voice called from the distance, "Wake up, Nuala. Please, please wake up," She slowly turned and the *Banshees* were fading away.

Opening her eyes, she discovered to her amazement that she was in her own bed. What a nightmare, she thought with a shudder. Then she noticed that the girl who had given them the *Banshee* book was now standing beside her bed.

"Get up, Nuala, please, and wake the others," she said in an urgent voice. "The room above this is on fire – you are all in great danger."

Nuala stumbled from her bed and out of her cubicle; the air was filled with smoke. Dropping to her knees, she crawled towards the back wall of the room.

Feeling her way along the wall, she soon reached the place where the fire alarm box was located. Standing up again, she stretched for it, choking, and blinded by the smoke which was pouring in under the door from the tower staircase. Somehow she managed to break the glass and press the button. This, she knew, would set the whole system of alarm bells ringing throughout the castle.

Gasping for air, she leant against the wall, wondering how she would ever get to the door of the main dormitory through the dark cloud of acrid smoke which surrounded her. Someone loomed up beside her. It was the girl again.

"Well done, Nuala," she said warmly. "Follow me. I'll lead you to safety. Judith has called the others."

Nuala followed the girl, rubbing her streaming eyes with a pyjama sleeve as she did so. When they reached her own cubicle again, the atmosphere was much clearer there, so Nuala darted in, picking up her dressing gown and her talking watch, shuffling into her slippers at the same time.

When she joined the others, she discovered a scene of great confusion. Aileen, blindly dragging on her dressing gown, had bumped into Josie, causing her to drop some cherished objects belonging to Ciara, who was weeping uncontrollably, while Deirdre was running around in circles calling, "Let's get out of here, let's get out of here."

"This way, and hurry up please," called a clear firm voice.

Nuala and Judith saw their rescuer standing in the doorway leading to St Anne's dormitory. Quickly they urged Aileen and the others through it. Once inside, they joined the girls there who were waiting for the prefect to give the order to leave the room as soon as she had checked that everyone was accounted for.

Nuala, who was last in the line, turned to thank the girl who had saved them. The girl was standing with her back to the closed door of Annie's Pocket, through the sides of which Nuala could see that wisps of smoke were already appearing.

"Aren't you coming with us?" Nuala asked in surprise.

The girl smiled then shook her head.

Judith came and joined Nuala. "Who are you?" she burst out. "What's your name, you must tell us?"

"We'd really like to know," said Nuala "After all, you've saved our lives."

The girl smiled again. "It was the least I could do to thank you," she said softly "You see, my name is Elizabeth Bruder, and you cleared it for me."

They were astonished to see her point to something shining brightly on her dress. They recognised it at once. It was the *Merry Gold Medal* with *E Bruder 1896* engraved on it.

As they stood in stunned silence gazing incredulously at her, her face seemed to grow brighter and brighter.

"I'm going away now," she said in a happy voice. "Thank you again!"

Then she was gone. Her voice seemed to linger on the air and it sounded as if she were saying *Alter Ipse Amicus.*

A loud crashing noise could be heard from Annie's Pocket. It sounded as if the ceiling had fallen in, at least.

"Come on, you two," shouted the prefect impatiently. "What's keeping you? Do you want us all to be burned alive?"

Nuala and Judith never said a word, just hurried over and walked out of the dormitory, closely followed by the prefect. They ran down the stairs, joining the girls who were streaming out of the main entrance of the castle.

It was only when they arrived out in the cold night air full of the noise of fire engines and raised voices giving orders that Judith broke the silence between them.

"I can't get over it," she whispered "While we were all watching the *Why Cases,* and even some girls casting spells as witches, a real ghost was going around the castle at the same time, and no one even realised it!"

Nuala squeezed her arm, and whispered back. "It makes you think, doesn't it? I'm glad we saw her. She was so happy, I'll never be afraid of ghosts again!"

THE END